M000029513

Faith Set Free

A Memoir

Barbara Hall Gemar

*"My heart is inditing a good matter; I speak of the
things which I have made touching the king: my tongue
is the pen of a ready writer."* **Psalm 45:1 (KJV)**

A Ready Writer
Johnson City, Tennessee

Copyright © 2019 by Barbara Hall Gemar
ISBN 978-1-5136-5306-8 (print)
ISBN 9781688284111 (KDP)

Genre: Fictional Memoir

Faith Set Free: A Memoir is a fictional narrative based on a true story. It reflects the author's present recollections of experiences over time. Some names and characteristics have been changed, some events have been compressed and some dialogue has been recreated.

All scripture quoted within this book comes from the King James Version since the author and her audience are most familiar with that version. If the quotation is from a different version, it is otherwise noted. "In 1604, King James I of England authorized that a new translation of the Bible into English be started. It was finished in 1611, just 85 years after the first translation of the New Testament into English appeared (Tyndale, 1526). The Authorized Version, or King James Version, quickly became the standard for English-speaking Protestants. Its flowing language and prose rhythm has had a profound influence on the literature of the past 400 years. The King James Version present on the Bible Gateway matches the 1987 printing. The KJV is public domain in the United States." (Versions, King James Version, 2019)

All rights reserved. No part of this book may be reproduced without permission by the publisher with the exception of a reviewer, who may quote brief passages in a review; nor may any part of this book be stored in a retrieval system or recorded (by mechanical means, photocopying or other) without permission from the author at barbara@areadywriter.ink

A Ready Writer | Johnson City, Tennessee

Front Cover Photo: Payton Studio, Colorado Springs, Colorado
Back Cover Photo: David Gemar
Original Artwork: Daniel Cook, based on images
Book Cover Design: Clark Kenyon

For the people whom God used

to emancipate me

from my Emmanuel background

through lessons of bondage or freedom.

Etymology

For ten years the working title of this book was *"Emmanuel Emancipation: The Story of a Girl Set Free"*. At the time of this printing, those words seem archaic for a shelf in a bookstore. Yet, they so perfectly describe this book that they are worth mentioning here to further explain the context of this story.

Immanuel noun
Im·man·u·el | \ i-ˈman-yə-wəl , -yəl\
variants: or *Emmanuel*
Definition of Immanuel: MESSIAH sense 1
First Known Use of Immanuel
15th century, in the meaning defined above

History and Etymology for Immanuel
Middle English Emanuel, from Late Latin Emmanuel, from Greek Emmanouēl, from Hebrew ʾimmānūˈēl, literally, with us is God (dictionary/immanuel, 2019)

emancipate verb
eman·ci·pate | \ i-ˈman(t)-sə-ˌpāt \
emancipated; emancipating
Definition of emancipate
transitive verb

1 : to free from restraint, control, or the power of another especially : to free from bondage
2 : to release from parental care and responsibility and make sui juris
3 : to free from any controlling influence (such as traditional mores or beliefs) (dictionary/emancipate, 2019).

Table of Contents

Prologue

"And ye shall know the truth, and the truth shall make you free" (John 8:32, King James Version). Sometimes we awaken to surroundings that we realize are unusual, but we are not aware because they have been our only reality for so long. Such was the story of Bridget and Priscilla who grew up in a culture completely controlled by the authority of their church. It was as if what really worked well for churches in the late thirties and forties became frozen in time, and the church forefathers of that era, who founded the Emmanuel Circle of Churches, permanently decreed the minute details for life and godliness. These decrees continued with success for the rest of the century. Their motives were pure, and their message was not all bad but harsh enough to be destructive. In many cases, as in the lives of Priscilla and her family, this hardship was a "schoolmaster to bring [them] to Christ".

"Wherefore the law was our schoolmaster to bring us unto Christ, that we might be justified by faith" (Galatians 3:24).

The rules and regulations of the church were rooted in words from the Bible, but there was a fine line between the good of the rules and the control of the leadership. That was what damaged the thinkers who could not succumb to the entirety of the written code.

The Emmanuel Circle of Churches had begun with some preachers coming out of a denomination known as the Pilgrim Holiness Church and aligned doctrinally with what was originally Wesleyan theology. While this theology clearly taught salvation by faith alone in Christ alone, there was the additional expectation that a person should go on to holiness or sinless perfection, thus living a life on this earth completely free from sin. As a side effect of this belief, any departure from sinless perfection would bring a person right back to where they started again; as a sinner in need of forgiveness and seeking another definitive experience of salvation. No matter if there had been any prior experience as a believer in Christ, death in the moment after a sin would result in direct banishment to hell for all eternity.

Frequent mandatory meetings kept the followers tight-knit, and ideologies thrived in an environment cut off from the outside world. Yes, the people still needed to shop in the local grocery store or buy gasoline at the service station. Banks, power companies and work were still a part of daily living but even work had its restrictions: Never work on Sunday. Don't wear a uniform unless it complies with the dress standard of the church. Never join the military. Participation in team sports—or watching them from a stadium—was sinful.

The greatest motivator in the Emmanuel Circle of Churches was fear. If people could be made afraid, they could be controlled. If they could be controlled, they would not think for themselves If they thought for themselves, they may question the entire establishment and questioning would lead to its demise.

For over forty years the system worked well. It grew and became known throughout the United States, Ireland, Africa and Guatemala. Young people were drawn to its purity and the ambassadors who recruited for the Bible School were successful. Here young people would come in their middle to late teens and finish high school, then go on to four years of college. Cloistered in the confines of a beautiful campus with men's and women's dormitories, their own print shop producing approved literature, a dining room, private laundry facilities, church and classrooms,, their world was complete. Careers included preaching, teaching, construction and the occasional factory or city worker. Women had a choice of teaching, caregiving, housecleaning for other people and being a pastor's wife. Some families continued farming.

Several shattering events occurred in the eighties and nineties which forced Priscilla to make some difficult decisions. This is the story of how her family walked through those challenges and how their faith emerged on the other side.

Though there are many respected characters in this story who are still living, all names have been changed to protect their identities. While not written from an omniscient perspective, I simply recall events as they are remembered, with the purpose of bringing hope to anyone else who is bound by confusion and fear wondering if they, too, may be set free.

Part I

Early Years

Nebraska Autumn

"Yes, Lovey, Mamma is coming. Let me put the lid on this last jar," Margaret soothed from the kitchen. Baby Bridget was starting to whimper so Frank rocked her in the wooden chair with its back and seat softly covered in brown leather. "I will tuck you in, if you can just give me a moment," Margaret called out, as Frank lulled Bridget into slumber.

"There's a land beyond the river—" Frank began to sing in his mellow bass voice as he rocked backward and forward, the fresh smell of wood shavings from the lumberyard on his jeans.

Margaret stirred the apple butter on the stove, reaching over her expanding tummy. It was a brisk, fall night, and she felt the familiar nesting instinct as she preserved the Jonathan apples from the neighbor's tree.

The sun had already slid beyond the plateaus of the western horizon, and the bright stars that twinkled above the quiet town spoke peace to the little family in the white frame house on the corner. Frank, thankful to be home from his job an hour away, knew Bridget would soon be asleep in her crib. There she would be dreaming of her first birthday cake in three weeks.

"Frankie," sighed Margaret, "do you suppose this baby has dropped?" She was referring to the maternal stirring of the slow-moving little person inside her, but this time it felt different. Lower. Stronger. A little bit more urgent.

"Maybe I just need to lie down and rest my back," she muttered to herself after tucking in Bridget. Frank lay reading "Barnes' Notes on the New Testament" by Albert Barnes, when she snuggled down beside him for a few hours of sleep.

"I don't know," his tender voice replied from behind his book. "But remember, I am right here if you need anything." Looking across the pillows into her hazel eyes, Frank smiled that deeply contented smile that comes from a lover who believes his treasure was worth the wait.

The following morning, the family slid into the handsome '64 Ford Falcon to pick up some last-minute baby items at JCPenney's. Once outside, Margaret went to step off the curb and knew that she could not return home that day.

Firmly grasping the parking meter outside the store, she asked Frank to take her to St. Elizabeth's Hospital instead. There, a few hours later, a healthy baby girl was born with a slightly-smooshed left eye as a result of her rocky passage into the world. Softly caressing her tufts of brown hair, Frank and Margaret bent over their new little girl and named her Priscilla Maureen after a missionary to Africa and a beloved aunt in England. All memory of pain was quickly forgotten with the joy of the births of Bridget and Priscilla, eleven months apart, which had increased the population of their town in southwestern Nebraska from two hundred to two hundred and two.

Priscilla was a calm baby with a long attention span as she watched the world around her. As soon as her grandmother, Mrs. Watkins in West Virginia, learned of her birth, she boarded a Greyhound bus and traveled all night to care for her son's first-born child in the wake of Priscilla's arrival. Bridget was only eleven months old and would need some mothering during this transition. When Mrs. Watkins reached the back door of the parsonage many hours later, she reached into her purse and pulled out a clean cloth and a bottle of Lysol. Carefully, she disinfected the bottom of her shoes before she entered the vulnerable environment of her new granddaughter's home. She loved her family so much and had experienced many sacrifices through the years to be where she was that day.

Quickly, Mrs. Watkins took over the responsibilities of the household so that her daughter-in-law could heal and focus on the needs of her new baby. Margaret spent many hours cuddling both girls on her lap as she nursed Priscilla. Mrs. Watkins remarked on the nurturing capabilities of her daughter-in-law and continued to cook, clean and wash to make the work of the little home go forward.

In the meantime, Frank was hard at work during the day, driving the long distance to and from the lumberyard and sequestering himself away at night in the upstairs study. There, he prepared his sermons for the upcoming Sunday or prayer meeting on Wednesday night. His main responsibility was the pastorate made up of four women and his own family. They would meet three times a week in the old Eddy schoolhouse out in the country. The schoolhouse had been converted into a small country church. Though it had no running water and the parishioners used an outhouse, it still had a special charm about it despite its primitive appearance. It was clean and painted inside and out, complete with a piano, pulpit and altar in front. The dull hardwood of the floor made a clacking sound against Margaret's pumps as she walked to play the piano for every service. Though busy in ministry and working at the lumberyard, Frank was always faithful to soothe babies or help with the home as much as he could. Margaret served him award-winning cakes, cinnamon rolls, nutritious dinners, and sweet companionship as his wife.

Priscilla's little life was off to a solid start with joy, security and peace surrounding her. In time, she would grow more aware of her heritage, but for now, she was singularly blessed by a legacy of love and faith from the lives of her parents and grandparents.

The Immigration

In 1952, the Georgic ocean liner sailed from Cobh Harbor in Ireland, across the Atlantic Ocean to New York City in the United States of America. Margaret, the brunette, fair-skinned Irish girl, second of eight children, was the first to step onto American soil. She had come with her two brothers and five sisters, her parents and the housekeeper, with one purpose in mind. They were traveling to a Bible school, where her parents intended to improve the education and environment for the family. Margaret was vivacious, extremely bright, musical and a bit given to a melancholy nature. She was a joyful follower of Jesus, who she believed had brought her to this new land and had changed her attitude toward her parents. She loved the Lord and enjoyed his words in the Bible. It was easy for her to make friends, and she was a very hard worker for her family.

Her father had been a diligent entrepreneur in

Dublin and sought to live a righteous life by adhering to the faith of the Methodist church he and his wife attended. He was kind, though strict, and loved his children deeply. His grandfather had left Baden-Württemberg, a southwest German state, with only a Bible and a silver coin and traveled to England. Later, his son emigrated to Dublin and started a pork-butchering business into which Margaret's father was born.

Though small and fragile, Margaret's mother was a spirited little lady who could manage the household from her bed, if necessary, where she often retired from the chaos of her lively children. She took schoolwork and the arts very seriously and was a woman of good works, especially to those in need. Leaving all that was familiar, with children ranging in ages from fifteen years to eight months, was a daunting adventure. Her plucky disposition was up for it, and though her hair was pure white when she made the journey, she never lost the sparkle in her brown eyes that told of her youthful spirit.

Meanwhile, up along the mouth of Campbell's Creek in a holler' near Charleston, West Virginia, two brave young people had started a home in 1934.

Frank's father, Stanley Watkins, was a stoic carpenter who worked on the barges that were used for carrying coal to maintain the mining industry, up and down the Kanawha River. He had left school in third grade to work and never was able to return.

Married to lovely Dorcas Watkins, who had a keen sensitivity for understanding people, the Watkins worked very hard to provide for their three children. Though the coal dust affected Stanley's lungs and he later acquired emphysema, he used that forced slow-down to offer him time to read and reflect. He always had his Bible nearby and loved to go to the local Holiness church. He also freely imparted his life's wisdom to anyone who would respectfully listen.

Of Cherokee Indian princess descent, Dorcas Watkins was a gorgeous lady with dark brown eyes and long brown braids wound about her head like an artistic pie crust edging. She never stopped. Cleanliness and history were her passions and wherever she lived, she shined it up like a hospital surgery suite. She was the oldest of thirteen children and had left school in fifth grade to help provide for the family. Her mind never atrophied as she voraciously read everything she could lay her hands on about her beloved country. She loved postcards that documented special places and kept intricate albums on specific themes, events and locations. Her heart was as huge as the universe and she loved people but hated sin. She could cook a banquet on a dime and raced around the house in her pumps, from one chore to the next, with purpose and peace. Sentimental but wise, she was a rock to all who sought refuge in her friendship. When she had been married sixty-four years, her granddaughter asked how she stayed married for so long.

"Well, I learned early on that I didn't want to hang around the women who ran down their husbands," she replied. That decision had served her well and given her the determination to be faithful and loyal to her Stanley.

When their son, Frank, was seventeen he also made the trek out west to attend Bible school. He had only been in town a couple of weeks when he saw a beautiful young girl across the church on the ladies' side of the aisle. He was impressed with that fourteen-year-old girl and could not get her out of his mind. Her virtue and beauty had him smitten, and after waiting eight years, he finally received permission from the president of the college to meet

Margaret in the Tower Room of the church during a break in the school's class schedule.

The Tower Room bore a resemblance to a square steeple in the front corner of the church where the students had their daily chapel services and worshipped with others in the community on Sundays. It was at the back of the church sanctuary, and a curving staircase brought one to the mystical top floor.

At Christmastime, a record player sent beautiful sounds of carols across the crunchy snow below as the music slipped through the open windows and out into the icy, mountain night air. Such was the tradition of school Christmas programs and special services.

Up to this Tower Room, Margaret climbed one spring afternoon and waited. Frank was on his way, ascending the stairs to see the girl of his dreams and he was planning to ask her if her feelings for him were mutual. As he opened the door and started upstairs, his heart nearly clogged his throat as it continued to beat, and his hands grew damp. He was soon at the top of the stairway, and there she stood, a lacy, white handkerchief in her right hand. To his total delight, their feelings were mutual, and he now knew that he would eventually be able to date her and maybe even to ask for her hand in marriage. During this time, Margaret was experiencing great loss and suffering on the home front. Her beloved father, who had sold everything he had to bring his family to America from Dublin, Ireland, was battling multiple myeloma cancer. Starting with a small knot on his leg that did not heal after a simple bump and bruise, the family soon learned that the father who had given everything for them was about to give the ultimate sacrifice: his life.

They had been in America for eight years, and the oldest girls were finishing college and starting their teaching careers. One had even married. However, still at home were the seven remaining children, down to the youngest eight-year-old. After his short career of working in their new life in America, Margaret's father was going to die. She had started working in the hospital that summer and felt very close to him in his final hours. He loved his children to the very end and his death left an indelible imprint on each unique individual.

Emily, the brave mother of Margaret, made the difficult choice to go out to look for a job to support her precious family. The girls sewed, cleaned house, and cared for others in their efforts to pull together and provide for each other. The teenage boys found work for local landscaping jobs and construction projects, and Emily began care-giving in hospitals and nursing homes. Her gentle hands and perky spirit made her a favorite in the community, and she kept it up until the last few years of her life.

During those difficult times of suffering and loss, character was developed in each of the children and Margaret had the distinct joy of knowing that her father knew of her newfound love in Frank, and he had given her his blessing. She looked forward to the day when she would be in Frank's arms to enjoy the security of his love as long as God gave them life.

When Frank took Margaret as his bride in the very place of worship where he had stated his love for her five years before, the May afternoon was bathed in bright sunshine. A stiff breeze played with Margaret's veil and red-rose bouquet, but she had eyes only for her beloved Frank.

That evening they headed up the mountain pass to a tiny, rustic cabin for their honeymoon. Priscilla's home was begun that day, and her parents were closely following the God whose will had brought them together.

After six years of theological studies, Frank was ready to take his first pastorate in southeastern Colorado. There he served in a dusty town, surrounded by locusts, sugarcane farmers, and constant wind. Memories there included their first pet, a lively Cocker Spaniel puppy.

With sadness, they assisted in the funeral of a newborn baby of dear college friends who laid their little one to rest. It was also in this lonely spot that Frank and Margaret learned they were going to be parents for the first time. Shortly following, Frank was called to pastor in Nebraska.

The Happy Golden Years

The move to the Midwest was a perfect one for Frank and Margaret as they took their belongings and moved along with their baby who would be born the following year. The years living there were often referred to as "The Happy Golden Years". In a tiny town where everyone knew each other, there was great community support and a healthy atmosphere for doing business.

Into this home was born their first child, a lively, intelligent girl named Bridget. She was deeply bonded to her mother and quickly advanced in walking and talking. At times, she would even finish the sentences out loud that her mother was silently thinking. Even though their hearts were full of joy with this delightful little human, they easily found room for their second daughter, Priscilla, born eleven months later.

Every morning, Margaret would take the little girls to the post office to pick up the mail. They would get out the aqua, steel stroller and walk there and back. They knew the banker and where he lived because Frank had painted for him at his summer cabin.

Nothing survived or failed without the entire town recognizing the event. When the wheat crops were destroyed with hail, the entire town would drive to the edge and comfort the farmers. When a baby was born, everyone would stop to rejoice. The bank had a special silver spoon engraved for Priscilla, including the date and time she was born, precisely shown on a tiny round clock. Should a baby bunny need a hutch, someone would swing around the corner in a pickup truck and provide one. When a tornado was predicted to come through, each neighbor looked out for the next to be sure there was safety. At harvest time, the town's people gathered by the edge of the wheat fields to watch the combines arrive and cut the wheat.

Western sunsets are breathtaking over the barren plains and rough plateaus of western Nebraska. No trees dot the landscape and the horizon seems to be made up of only land and sky. Cottonwood and elm trees can be found near some of the riverbeds or in established towns but other than that there is not much to break up the familiar scenery. Prairie dogs, pheasants and meadowlarks can be found unexpectedly sharing the plains with humans.

The rhythm of the days included order and constant industry. Margaret worked hard keeping the little house immaculate and rejoiced that her floors were always so clean that the little girls who crawled across them in white stockings never showed a lick of dirt on their little knees. In addition, she washed and polished their walking shoes every night to remove any scuffs from the white toes.

The little girls and their mother only wore homemade dresses that were designed with specific patterns required by Church. Only fabrics that were muted colors such as lavender, mint and various shades of pink and blue were acceptable. In the winter, darker colors such as brown, black or dark green and navy were used. They were never allowed to wear red, yellow or purple. These colors were considered too bright and were "worldly".

Frank's clothing was not so restricted; apart from always being meticulously clean-shaven with a short haircut, Frank could buy his clothing as long as he wore dark pants and plain, button-down long-sleeved shirts with no pattern in the fabric. Ties could only be black or very dark navy.

Cars were regulated as well with certain colors banned and other features such as sidewalls, windows without a steel rim around the door, and stripes along the side prohibited. Even though there were many regulations from the "Guidebook" of the Emmanuel Circle of Churches, Frank and Margaret abided by the rules with an odd contentment.

The ethical standards of conduct cited in the Bible School's rulebook prohibited rowdyism, profanity, the use of tobacco, alcoholic beverages or drugs, card playing, gambling, dancing and the attendance of places of worldly amusement such as theaters, movies, circuses, fairs, carnivals, intercollegiate games and other kindred pastimes – "[All are] strictly forbidden. Students are not permitted to have radios or television sets."

The radio or television were not allowed in any home or car throughout the organization and music could only be Christian or classical. The church reserved the right "to inspect any literature, records, or tapes that are in the possession of any student, and to ban those that are not in harmony with the ethical standards and ideals of the School." (General

Council of the Emmanuel Association, 1984)

One peculiar guideline was that of women needing to sew a lateral seam across the cups of any purchased bra to minimize any curvature or fullness. A meeting was held in the church, for women only, to fully explain the intricate details of modest dressing. Perhaps it was their very exclusion that kept members of them so isolated that they were not even aware of how much they were different.

Six times a year special church services were held in regional areas. There was a two-week revival in the early spring when an evangelist would come and preach every night and twice on Sundays. Several weeks later, a four-day convention with three services a day was held both in the east and west of the United States. In the summer, there was a camp meeting in both the east and the west that lasted ten days with four services each day. Additional morning and evening prayer meetings separated the men and women.

Special children's services were held each day as well. The church services were tedious while the children endured many hours of sitting and were not allowed to wiggle or turn around. No "nursery" or children's program existed other than the half hour each evening when a very kind, elderly man with elbow-walking sticks would take his place at the front of the tabernacle on a chair in the wood shavings and tell Bible stories a child would never forget.

Along with some cheerful children's songs and a short prayer, this was the extent of the children's ministry at the camp meetings each summer. Children were often taken outside the building to a car to be spanked so that they would sit still and quiet. They were disciplined in the car so their cries would not reach the people remaining in the tabernacle for the service.

The doctrine of the church taught the tenets of the evangelical faith, but there was a significant emphasis on a second work of grace known as sanctification that would occur after the experience of salvation. Because the believer worked so hard through seeking and confession to obtain this salvation, the standard remained high, and the requirements for Godly living to maintain them were impeccable.

It was easy to believe a person had lost their salvation and needed to become a Christian all over again. This conviction caused untold anxiety among some of the tender-hearted believers and their Christian walk was filled with fear and a lack of assurance. Confession was a regular part of the services, when people would stand to their feet and state a specific way that they had fallen short of perfection and were seeking to be cleansed from that particular sin. Sometimes it was for running up the stairs two at a time or for having pride or jealous attitudes toward another person. These statements were usually accepted from the leadership and often encouraged as requirements for a deeper work of God's grace.

Because Frank and Margaret had both come into the church as teenagers, they had some memories of a Christian faith outside of the church. Their memories were based on Bible truths from other Christians in their past, pointing them to Jesus instead of to a specified rule in a book.

Frank's Christian heritage dated back to his mother and father who were married by a Pilgrim Holiness pastor in 1934. In those early years, Stanley, Frank's father, was a minister of the Gospel and carried a small book for conducting weddings and funerals. His hunger for righteousness led him to the simple faith of his bride, Dorcas, and her devotion to

God and obedience to His word directed her mothering. She was quick to take in a hurting neighbor or fatherless child. She loved her own children so completely that there was little opportunity for them to stray from her tenderness and care. Even when Frank was seventeen and on his way to Bible school in Colorado, it was hard for him to unwrap the sandwich his mother had caringly wrapped for him. It was equally hard to throw away the paper even after he had eaten it because it was from her hands. This nest of a loving introduction to faith held Frank steady through the later years of legalism, rules and seeking his own path toward Biblical truth.

Now with his growing family, where Frank was the pastor of the little church, he was able to study deeply in the scriptures and deliver messages that were fresh from his time with God. He studied commentaries and theology with a passion and his reading of biographical works such as John Wesley, Amanda Smith, Samuel Logan Brengle, Brother Lawrence and others offered fresh inspiration to his little flock. This kept a positive balance in the spiritual life of the family as they lived from day to day apart from the intense larger meetings of revival, convention and camp meetings that occurred throughout the year. Through the ordinary days, an opportunity always existed for showing the love of God as they shared their lives with the community, including those for whom Frank did extra painting or carpentry jobs on the side.

The church congregation of four women was unique. Mrs. McMillard was a smiling, white-haired lady, with a big heart, who lived across the street from the Watkins family. It was a great help to have this experienced Christian neighbor there whenever young Margaret needed an immediate grandmother or friend.

Miss Lombard lived in town in a tiny little house and had a bristly chin that brushed across the little girls' cheeks whenever she gave them a kiss. On the other side of town lived Mrs. Current, a busy lady who had a lot of common sense as a retired farmer's wife. She was very like Mrs. Croft who also lived in town. Some of the ladies were picked up for church and rode with Frank and Margaret and their babies each time a service was held.

Margaret worked hard keeping up with her two little ones. Often one cloth diaper would be freshly changed when the other one needed to be and as soon as that was done the first baby's diaper was dirty and it began all over again.

The kitchen and sewing machine seemed to be where Margaret spent most of her time, stitching simple little dresses and bonnets, slips, woolen coats and hats. She also made aprons and dresses for the little girls and herself. Her boundless creativity found expression in these everyday tasks and she enjoyed repurposing the perfect wool of a slightly worn coat towards a coat for the girls, warmly lined with a flannel receiving blanket from when they were tiny.

Reading was a lifelong love of Margaret's and when the girls were old enough to not need round-the-clock, full-time care, she would steal off to the local library of the tiny village and borrow the key from the lady who was the Keeper of the Books. Once inside the library, Margaret would make further selections of literature which she had not yet had an opportunity to read: "War and Peace" and "Anna Karenina" by Leo Tolstoy, "Letters Home" by Sylvia Plath and others. Her voracious appetite for reading led her into many different genres, but her conscience was a careful guide.

Once she was convicted of reading a certain

collection that she did not believe was truly spurring her on towards a holy life, so she quickly took those books out of the house and returned them to the library that very afternoon. Nobody would have known, but her children did! And they did not forget, either. It was a tiny lesson with great implications for teaching integrity.

There was a garden plot as well that Frank carefully tended. He was discouraged by the dryness of the climate compared to the well-watered hills of West Virginia. It gave him greater understanding for the farmers' dependence on the rain and lack of hail and wind for success.

Some fascinating experiences occurred along the twenty-mile ride out to Eddy schoolhouse. One hot summer evening Frank found a rattlesnake stretched across the road sunning himself in the dust. The innate hunting instinct came over Frank and he just had to put the snake to an immediate death with stones thrown from the roadside. Pulling to the side of the road, Frank killed it and took out his pocketknife. He deftly clipped the rattlers off the snake and wrapped them neatly in tissue, placing it in a Vicks box to mail to his father. Each hunter must show off his trophy, right?

Bunnies

What child does not dream of a soft, cuddly bunny to hold? These girls did, too, and they were overjoyed when their daddy brought home a white, red-eyed Bunny Button for their first pet. Frank constructed rabbit hutches behind the back of the garage and the little girls had their first introduction to the cycle of life. They stood at the hutch those warm spring days while they watched Bunny Button at eye-level. The water and food pellets had the most interesting way of being processed day after day and always looking the same.

Soon, another bunny came to join them who was coal-black. Her name was Blacky and Blacky and Bunny Button belonged to Priscilla and Bridget, respectively. Blacky seemed smaller than Bunny Button because she was the female.

One Sunday morning as Frank returned from feeding the rabbits, he walked up to the house with a big smile on his face holding up two fingers. There were two baby bunnies in the cage and the whole family was excited. By the time they returned from church there were more, and all were a little overwhelmed by the fun and responsibility of the children's first baby pets.

The sun continued to get warmer and a few days later, when Frank went to feed the bunnies, he found they had tragically died. They were just too hot and could not live in the direct sunshine.

There were tears that day, but a lesson was learned about the circle of life and the practical importance of shade for living things on the hot plateaus of western Nebraska. Frank lovingly dug a grave for the little bunnies and carefully buried them when the girls were not watching so that they would not be further hurt.

One of the best parts of the little house on the corner was the clothesline. It afforded a regular visit outside on cold winter days for three young ladies to get some fresh air. Margaret was always careful to bundle everybody up in warm clothes and as she hung the laundry on the line, every piece was sorted according to color and type of clothing. The little white panties were all hung together according to size. The sheets were stretched across the line with the set from which they had come and dried quickly in the stiff breeze. Sometimes Margaret would bring out a kitchen chair for Bridget to stand up on when she wanted to help.

There was a big storage area across the front of the house where the main entrance had been in years past. It was called "the storeroom" and was a delightful place to explore when the little girls were bored. They were always intrigued by how cold it was in the winter and how hot it was in the summer. It was dusty and filled with boxes of Christmas decorations, wedding mementos and Margaret's accordion. She would pull it out for Christmas programs to play as accompaniment to the carols. In that curious room, she also kept the love letters, tied in a pink ribbon, that Frank had mailed to her during their lengthy courtship. There were college notebooks and numerous teaching resources that she had collected from her years of study and teaching before she had her own children.

The kitchen was another wonderful resource in which Margaret expressed her creativity. Some days it was a double-layered orange cake with orange icing. Other days it was homemade crescent rolls arranged equidistantly on the Mirro cookie sheet.

At Christmas she would pull out her cookie press and make tiny butter cookies in the shapes of wreaths and trees. They were perfectly baked without even the hint of brown on the edges and resulted in a melt-in-your mouth softness that dissolved on the happy recipient's tongue.

The hot summer evenings were eased with the ice cream freezer in which they made their signature vanilla recipe from the fresh cream of the local farmland. Frank would kneel by the hand-cranking machine for the entire batch while Margaret sat on a lawn chair and the girls chased lightening bugs.

Frank was creative, too, and the ready access to lumber made it easy for him to design and build a one-car garage. A huge cottonwood tree was taken down to make room for the building. The girls watched with fascination while the cement truck came to pour the floor and their daddy worked hard in the hot afternoon sun to smooth it perfectly. Then he made them smile at the end of the project when he wrote their initials and the date in the corner of the sidewalk, reminding them that there would always be a mark of their work that day.

He placed wooden windows, along with a small and large door in the garage and painted the exterior white. Inside he built custom shelves for the family to transfer some of their storage items yet keep their car shiny and unscratched.

Several other lessons of death occurred in those early years when a young high school student tried his first drink of alcohol and later that night was killed along with his friend in a car accident outside of town. How vivid that memory was the next morning as the girls and their daddy went out to the site of the accident where the car had not yet been removed.

Another time a small airplane crashed and burned with fatalities also leaving an indelible memory of the brevity of life. With Frank's somber, southern roots, he took death seriously and always paused to remember whenever those in the community would suffer.

Priscilla always liked excitement. She lived in a family of booky people and it just seemed there was never anyone to play with her. One evening after dinner, she excused herself and snuck back to the bedroom to get her purse. She also "muskratted" her hair (combed back the strands which had escaped her little brown braids) and created a "check" which was really but a slip of paper. Out the front door of the storeroom she crept without anyone realizing she was gone. Tripping along to the grocery store downtown that evening, Priscilla had one intention. She was going to buy Neapolitan ice cream for her beloved sister. When the little four-year-old rounded the corner, who should be coming her way but the biggest black dog in town. As he bounded down the street, she whipped around and started home as fast as her little legs could go. When she arrived inside squealing and crying her mother met her to find out where she had gone. After hearing a tearful outpouring of the details, Margaret sat down on the bed and bit her bottom lip. "That was not a wise thing to do, Priscilla. You never know who might have been out there to hurt you this time of the day. Never, ever run away like that again without telling me where you are. I shall have to punish you with a spanking, so lean over my knee." With a broken heart, Priscilla took her discipline and was relieved to be back in her mother's arms, even without the ice cream. She never forgot the fright of that dog that was sent to protect her by scaring her back home.

Though at times a very tearful child, Priscilla also had a huge capacity for enjoying beauty and imagining great things. It was her favorite pastime to ride round and round the perimeter of the backyard on her little red tricycle while telling stories to herself that she made up or singing spiritual songs. It was always very inspiring to her and made her feel free as a bird. One afternoon she was riding and singing while a huge western thunderstorm was rolling across the plains headed towards town. As her little heart exulted with the rising pressure in the air, these words came to her mind:

"Tucked up in hope,

Where the beautiful church stands."

On and on she sang about the little church and felt very poetic as she later repeated it for her mother. The early seeds of her love for writing were starting to sprout in the well-cultivated soil of her encouraging home.

Part II

When Reality Gives a Jolt

The Grey Elephant

As the little girls were growing up and Bridget turned five, Frank and Margaret felt that it was time to move to a different pastorate where the girls would be able to go to the local church school. With the four grandmotherly ladies of the church, it did not look like an Emmanuel school would be opening anytime soon, locally. The Emmanuel Circle of Churches did not allow anyone to attend a school unless it was operating under its auspices. This involved packing up all the memories of their life in Nebraska and moving across the country to northeastern Ohio. A big, grey, moving truck and two Bible-school boys came to help with the move. For years, the truck had been fondly referred to, by moving pastoral families, as "The Grey Elephant".

Moving into a huge, brown house on the edge of their new city was a completely different lifestyle for the Watkins family. The parsonage was surrounded by a huge lawn and bordered by a railroad track. Across the tracks was a dense wood. There were hedges, trumpet vines, towering sassafras trees and even a hill to sled upon.

The spacious dining room entry from the front porch had a sturdy feel with a mirrored buffet and matching dining table and chair set. There was a painted, grey piano against the wall. By the front door was a small telephone table with a black, rotary telephone. A matching chair made a great place for Margaret to keep in touch with her Irish mother.

To the left was a small parlor with glass bookshelves in which Frank kept his Bible study books. The bay window provided a perfect location for the yearly Christmas tree. There was a bedroom downstairs as well as a large kitchen and laundry room. Upstairs was a bathroom and three bedrooms with closets and little attic entryways in each closet.

The exciting part about this was the constant adventure of exploring the old house with support posts in the basement that were twelve by twelve inches in diameter. A vintage, wringer washing machine in the basement still worked perfectly, even though it was old. Once a part of Margaret's woven headscarf got caught in it, as she was preparing to hang the laundry outside during the winter. After they had moved into the parsonage, those huge support posts were a busy hotel for termites, discovered just in time before their support gave way to a tragedy.

The house was old, big, laden with antiques, character and lots of light. There were many wonderful nooks and crannies for daydreaming, reading, playing with dolls or imagining. While the dining room was simple with its tile floor, it afforded a skating rink for Bridget who sailed across the tile with rags tied on her feet in between sessions of curling up in a corner and reading "Hans Brinker and the Silver Skates" by Mary Mapes Dodge. It was also fun to grab her mother's pale blue skates and take off for the drainage ditch, down by the railroad tracks, when it was frozen solid. There she could skate in the icy northern weather and feel even more like the people in her story.

During the summer, Priscilla enjoyed gathering natural treasures for playing house, such as a daisy for a fried egg, grains from dry grasses for cereal and the oddity of a rabbit's tail to establish the famed "Rabbit Tail Park" under the maple tree. Complete with a park map and ranger station, this little recreational spot was so real that a sign was placed in the yard for all to see. Grandma and Grandpa Watkins and Aunt Sophie were already influencing Priscilla with their generous sharing of vacations in the state parks, enhancing a love of nature and the ability to observe its beauty.

Within walking distance up the country road was a little candy store. It was easy to get there from the new parsonage. Also, it was a special treat when extended family visited to stroll up there and buy some candy for two cents apiece.

During the first summer, the neighbor told Bridget and Priscilla where to pick some currants growing wild. They decided to sell them to other neighbors for twenty-five cents a pint. At the end of the day their daddy took them into the parlor and explained to them how to figure out ten percent of their earnings in order to give a tithe in the offering plate at church the next Sunday.

One of the saddest memories of summer was when Frank's older brother came to visit with his new wife and three children from a previous marriage. They were traveling back to Tennessee and made a trip out of their way to visit in northeastern Ohio. Frank and Margaret went out to the car with the girls and spoke to his brother and the family but would not invite them into their home because they were all wearing shorts and had experienced a divorce and remarriage. It made an indelible impression on Priscilla and in retrospect seemed like such a brainwashed way to respond to an actual blood relative, a brother no-less. It seemed that the arrogance and bigotry exhibited at that moment could only have done more harm than good.

Summer brought an opportunity to garden with an artistic seed packet from Gurrney's seed company, costing only a penny. The child with the straw hat and colorful flower garden on the front was inspiring to imaginative Priscilla. Bridget was the one who put in the disciplined, hard work after Priscilla's inspiration waned. The girls enjoyed planting their own little corner of their daddy's garden. The strawberries did well in the bright sunshine and the corn had plenty of room to grow.

In town, there was a simple white church with a school in the basement. It had wooden pews inside, and that was new for the little girls. They were amused because their little white-stockinged legs and black shoes stuck straight out from the pew where they sat on either side of their mother.

The church had some more variety here! There was tall Mrs. South, the matriarch of the church, who attended with her exquisite, even taller daughter, during the holidays from Bible school. Mrs. South always carried a perfectly ironed handkerchief and made sure that the folds fell away just right from the palm of her hand. She lived out in the country and had marvelous blueberry bushes that set the standard for that fruit for the rest of Priscilla's life. Mrs. South was an amazing cook and could make Lima Bean Soup taste perfectly gourmet. Even though she always had two mysterious cats somewhere in her house, there was not even the hint of cat odor with her Swedish cleanliness and standard of perfection.

One such visit to their home in the country, Bridget and Priscilla were getting restless with all the grown-up conversation. Mrs. South's daughter, home from college, took Priscilla by the hand and with her other hand drew a little map on Priscilla's tummy. "This is where you can go into my room to find some of my favorite books. You are looking for the 'Mother Westwind "Why" Stories by Thornton Burgess."

Mr. and Mrs. LouCassick also attended the

church for a short time and lived in another borough further away. Best of all they had dolls. The pastoral visits were so much more pleasant because of the small plastic people. One day, Mrs. LouCassick gave Bridget and Priscilla an ancient, forgotten china doll named "Lucy". She was in desperate need of a doll hospital. Margaret recognized this and carefully tucked away all her pieces in an old pillowcase at the bottom of a trunk. Eyeless Lucy with the matted hair traveled and remained in storage until a later time when she was restored by a qualified "doll doctor". She had new eyes, hair, had all her limbs "restrung" and Margaret made a beautiful turquoise satin dress for her with an overlay of ecru lace. She sat upon an antique footstool that could be turned up and down on a giant wooden screw and was a perfect hiding place for dollar bills.

The large snowflakes fell quickly as Frank drove the family out for pastoral calls that Thursday night. Priscilla was excited. She was going to get to see the home of her little friend, Katrina. Katrina had become near to her heart in October when she excitedly brought a white, plastic picture frame to school with a picture of a puppy on the inside. It was a birthday gift for Priscilla from her first childhood friend. She loved this little girl who was the youngest of eight children and whose father never attended church. Her mother told Priscilla gently that Katrina's father had trouble staying away from alcohol and that this made it hard for him to join the family at church. Priscilla loved Katrina's long, thin braids and brown dresses. She also felt compassion for her because it seemed her mother could not buy a new coat when she needed one. It was with excitement that the long journey into the snowstorm was made that night while "turkey tails" of flakes fanned across the front window.

At Katrina's house, the family piled out of the blue Ford and up the steps of the old farmhouse. How exciting to see their school friends in their own home! There was Donny with his square face and straight brown hair smiling broadly. Fred had a dimple in his cheek and shared second grade with Bridget. Sarah was there with her apron on, helping Bertha with the supper dishes and Rob came to the kitchen doorway displaying a roguish grin. Taller and in sixth grade, Bill had already stolen Priscilla's heart when he cut his finger at school and she gave him her first kiss on the hand from her tiny first-grade lips. How hard she had cried when she went home to talk with her mother about that terrible mistake! Her mother bit her lip shamefully, shifted her glance to the side and told Priscilla to never, ever do that again. No kissing in school or anywhere for that matter!

The most exciting event of all for the night was the unexpected pet at the family's home - a pet monkey! He was a busy little thing, called Mikey, and he swung from the stair banister to the top of the fireplace as if he owned the place. He even wore a little red coat that was just short enough to give considerable berth to his tail.

The teachers were always good about being involved in the outdoor and indoor games that the children played. Outside was a lot of gravel surrounding the church and school building and that was where they all went for recess. "Every Man in His Den" was when every student drew a circle in the gravel with a stick and stayed in his or her den until someone came over and "dared" the student to come out of the den and tag them. Then they had to come and stay in that den. The person who had the biggest den with everyone tagged, won.

Another game was "Dare Base" where all the students were broken into two teams. The teams were separated from one end of the playground to the other and the game was played similarly to "Every Man in His Den". As one team member would creep away from the safety of the "base", he or she would try to "dare" a team member from the opposite base. They could potentially be captured to go back to the opposite base. There, with one foot perpendicular to the base and stretching out as far as possible into the playground, and with one arm extended, the captured team member could be rescued by anyone who could make it into the danger zone and safely tag the captured team member without getting tagged and captured.

While the days grew shorter, summer slid into autumn and with it came pleasant walks from the school to the Mahoning River to see the mallard ducks under the covered bridge. The students and teacher would walk from the little chapel on Canal Street towards the river, where the mist hovered in spooky billows around the covered bridge. Oak leaves carpeted the bank and water eddied around the smooth stones along the edge of the riverbed. Brilliant reds, yellows and many shades of green caressed the roof of the bridge creating a spectacular site. Bridget, Priscilla and her younger friend,

Belinda, rambled in the woods building forts with the fallen branches or listening to their teacher read from "Bird Life in Wington" by John Calvin Reid. The spongy surface of the forest floor seemed unpredictable at every step. The musty aroma of fungi and the twinge of spice produced by a crushed sycamore leaf added to the delight of an afternoon in the woods. Though the days grew icy in the little town, there was plenty of warmth in the hearts of the children and their school friends. With Christmas coming, there were gifts to make at school, parties to enjoy and a program to get ready for upstairs in the church above the school.

Since Sundays were very strictly kept as a Sabbath day in the Watkins home, one custom was the weekly afternoon nap. Starting at two o'clock p.m., everyone went to their bed and stayed there for at least two hours. Since Bridget and Priscilla shared a double bed, their naps were just under the wire according to the rules! They were not tired at all and it was excruciating to lie there perfectly silent for two hours without talking, so they devised a plan. Both loved to play the piano and they found that they could play a tune with their fingers on the other person's arm and then that person would have to guess the name of the song. Of course, these songs were usually hymns learned in church. When Bridget or Priscilla guessed the title, they were rewarded with a smile and a nod. Rules of "no talking" were not broken!

A positive tradition for each school year was to take a school trip to an educational factory, historical park or cultural center. One year the school trip was to The J.M. Smucker Company on Strawberry Lane in Orrville, Ohio. There the children got to don little paper hats that said "Smucker's" on the sides and take samples of jellies and jams in tiny jars. That same day they visited the woodcarver, Ernest Warther, at his museum in Dover, Ohio. Mesmerized by the intricacy of all his wonderful trains, they were each honored to receive a tiny wooden pliers, perfectly handcrafted while they watched.

The South family, who had the cats and blueberries, were very dear to Bridget and Priscilla's hearts. Mr. South was memorable in his kindness to the girls on a frightening fall night after their return from a church convention in Canada. This was a four-day long event, arduous with church services three times a day and all meals – breakfast, lunch and dinner – eaten together. The hosting Emmanuel church would go out into the community and request people to keep strangers in their homes during those four days, at no cost. They would rent the use of a large local church, not an Emmanuel church, to handle the cooking and dining room.

After one of these conventions, Margaret, had become very ill on the way home from Niagara Falls and lay upstairs in the bedroom, unable to open her eyes. After days without sleep, tremendous pressure from the church leaders for all to come to the altar to confess their sins and the sadness of a chronic disapproval from the church superintendent, it seemed her nerves had splintered; and she was in desperate need of immediate mental healthcare.

Priscilla was sure that her mother would be soothed by her stuffed, blue bunny with the silky, pink ears. She crept upstairs, into her mother's bedroom, where she was lying with her head turned away from the door. Priscilla gave her mother her bunny for comfort, but in Margaret's serious condition, she simply hurled the bunny across the room where it crumpled dismally in the corner. In that moment, Priscilla's heart was also hurled violently in rejection and it took many years of compassion and understanding to come to the place of letting the pain go with maturity and forgiveness.

While she was being whisked off to a state hospital, Bridget and Priscilla, six and five years old respectively, were crying as if their hearts would break. It was cold, dark and rainy when Mr. and Mrs. South appeared in the driveway. Mrs. South was one of the leading members in the church, but her husband chose to never attend with her. He stepped out of the car that night, got down on the wet sidewalk on one knee and opened his coat wide enough to place both Bridget and Priscilla inside. His large hollow cheeks trembled as a tear slid down to the ground. In an unforgettable instant, the girls felt comfort such as they would never forget. Sometimes God really does show up in human skin.

Christmas on the River

After the initial shock of Margaret's illness in October, Frank continued to pastor the little church despite his wife's tragic circumstances. The girls were juggled from one aunt to another and Grandma Emily, Margaret's mother, came for a few weeks to help. Margaret started to get better and was soon released from the hospital. The heavy medications and shock treatments had left her very weak and she would sit in the rocking chair with her chin on her hand and stare for hours. Frank realized that for the home to continue to function normally there would need to be some daily household support. He was working as a janitor at the local post office and the responsibilities of being the pastor for the small church and headmaster for the little private school did keep him busy. Christmas was coming and there needed to be a plan.

Margaret struggled with the new medications and lack of consistent mental health care available in those days. She became sicker again and by Christmas had to be readmitted back into the same hospital. This time, her condition was more severe because she did not recognize Frank when he came to see her. By December twenty-fourth, she was a bit more cognizant, and Frank decided to take the children down to West Virginia to be with his parents for Christmas. They needed a holiday after all, he concluded. Though his heart was breaking, he was helpless to heal his wife and bring her back to her vivacious self. Stopping by the hospital to say goodbye on the way out of town, the girls stayed in the car and watched their mother come to the eighth-floor window and wave at her family as they got ready to drive away. The hospital seemed enormous and steely in the bleak, winter afternoon light as the girls peered at the window from the locked door. A loving arm extended in a wave assured them they were still in her thoughts though she was weak and showed little emotion.

Seated at the steering wheel was Frank with Priscilla on the hump and Bridget on the passenger's side by the door. It was dark by now and the rain blackened the sky even more as they crossed the wide Ohio River. Then there was a strange sound.

Something like a sniffle. Then a stifled sob. As they forged over the bridge and drew closer to home in the dark night, Priscilla looked up at her beloved daddy's face. She could not see it. With his right hand on the steering wheel, Frank drove on ahead and placed his left hand with the palm facing out, up to the side of his cheek to hide his emotion. Priscilla's tears began to trickle down her face, too. There was that dear hand with the big scar he received as a toddler when he placed it on a hot stove by accident, burning it badly. How often she had clung to it for security in her short little life, memorizing its rugged texture. As she looked up, she realized even fathers felt overwhelmed sometimes. Quickly, she cuddled up next to Bridget, who was a source of comfort to her once again.

Grandma and Grandpa Watkins were ready. The lights were up on the rim of the Appalachian porch roof and the tree was glowing happily inside. A hot fire in the woodstove warmed Aunt Sophie as she sat in the old wooden rocker. Grandma had disinfected the bathroom, kitchen, hallway boards and all the bedrooms with her Lysol. There was a pile of freshly sawed wood by the back porch that would last until the next millennium. In the refrigerator were supplies that Grandpa had been laying in for a month. A ham. Pepsi. French onion dip. Two gallons of ice cream. Grandma had the porch table laden with a mince cake, freshly baked rolls, two pumpkin pies, a pecan pie and a chocolate cake. In addition, she pulled some of her home-canned strawberry jam, apple butter, chili sauce, pickles and beets off the top shelf in the kitchen. As she dashed around the kitchen in her pumps and un-gathered apron, she stopped to give hugs to all the family as they arrived. Smiling through her tears, she kissed the girls and her own grown son. Love was exuding from the very wallpaper along the Kanawha River that night, and how it soothed the broken hearts of the suffering family who had driven over from Ohio that day.

Camping and Crying

It was January and Frank stayed true to his word. One Saturday morning he came home from the airport, introducing the girls to a stern lady with a twisted face. Her name was Flossie and she had come to be the cook, homemaker, mother, nanny, friend and disciplinarian. Flossie took up residence in the far bedroom upstairs that looked out over the hill where the girls sledded in the winter and the meadow where they gardened in the summer. She was a good soul, never married and without any children. She had a way of combing her chestnut hair perfectly into a large brown barrette winding the remainder into a tidy figure-eight bun at the nape of her neck. She had been in a serious car accident which had done nerve damage to her face, thus leaving her with a whimsical twist to her cheek and eye.

Flossie was disciplined, devoted, dangerous and delightful in many ways. First rule of business?

Never enter her room uninvited. She worked hard those days and kept the big, old, house clean with delicious meals always on the table. In addition, she befriended Margaret and kept a wise balance of friend and housekeeper, careful to not overstep her boundaries. She respected Frank and never interfered with his work. She was so consistent you could have set your clock by the way she tiptoed through the girls' bedroom every morning at six o'clock a.m., with her black shoes and stockings, fully dressed with an ironed apron and her hair perfectly combed. She was heading downstairs to make breakfast and get Bridget and Priscilla off to school. She was indeed a blessing, filled with love and wisdom, even though the children thought she was rather fierce.

Easter came that year and Flossie was busy making something the day before the Sabbath. She was leaning over a half-circle mound of cake, piled with coconut-covered icing and a little hill of jellybeans. What was she making? Soon she took a pastry brush out of the drawer and pulled six bristles from it, placing them precisely on the sides of the half circle beneath some pink icing ears. Then, as the black jellybean eyes fell into place, the family smiled with delight at the perfect creation of an Easter Bunny cake for Sunday. What a tender and creative person to make something so special, just for the children!

With spring came the return of visits to the Mahoning River. One day the children had strolled along the bank for a while enjoying the fresh burst of breezes that carried the scent of apple blossoms and daffodils in the air. Suddenly they saw it – a mother duck nestled under a bush on a nest of eggs. This was all they needed to begin a weekly pilgrimage back to the covered bridge to check on Mrs. Duck and her little family. One day the oak leaves shuffled with the movement under her warm body. Five little ducks remained when she toddled off her perch for a drink from the nearby river. They continued to grow more each week and by the end of the month of May they could be seen swimming in a tidy "V" behind their fearless mother.

An annual event for the summer was the trip to camp meeting that occurred the last week of June and lasted through the fourth of July. Though it was fun for the children to be down in the hickory grove for ten days with all their friends, it was very stressful for many of the parents. All parishioners of the eastern part of the United States would travel to northwestern Kentucky for the annual camp meeting. Though there were still some tents, most of the families stayed in little cabins resembling a yurt that were white, frame structures, with no running water and limited electricity. The cabins had a bed for parents and bunk beds for the children. A simple table was used for water containers and a basin. There were usually two screened windows and a screened door with a wooden door that could be latched at night. Restrooms were upgraded outhouses on either end of the campground. A water pump was near each establishment. Most notable in the outhouses were the little plywood booths for mother and child, with an ample wood-carved seat for the mother, right beside a smaller opening for the fearful toddler who accompanied her, both behind the same door.

There were huge trees, mushrooms, moss, rocks, flowers and many other collectibles for all the children to display at their cabin door. There was a hierarchy of who lived where. Unmarried men and women stayed in separate dorms that were more like Army barracks with rows of beds. Families who were not pastors or teachers stayed in tents. Pastors or teachers and their families stayed in cabins. For those who were superintendents or distinctive leaders within the association, there was running water with a bathroom and shower in their cabin. They were also the elite who ate at the Preachers' Table in the dining room. While the rest of the people lined up outside in the hot sun to wait for entrance to the dining hall, the privileged members of the Preachers' Table were able to directly access a table set with linen. They enjoyed better food, such as bacon and eggs, while the rest of the dining room looked on over the tops of their oatmeal and prunes.

The schedule began with an early-morning prayer meeting which parents were expected to attend. Mid-morning there was a worship service beginning at ten and lasting until noon or later, if there was an altar service. After lunch was quiet hour before a two-o'clock service again which lasted until four o'clock. The children often did not go to this because they would stay back for a nap. There was a children's service in the evening at six o'clock, which preceded the evening service at seven o'clock. Sometimes the altar services in the evening would last until midnight or later. These were times of praying, confession, exhortation, singing, more praying and confession and going to one another to correct each other or ask forgiveness. Such modeling of introspection caused Priscilla to constantly question her motives and thoughts at a very early age. Fearful of sinning and even more afraid of not being accepted by all the big people around her impressed her delicate conscience as a rubbing on a rock.

There was a mixed outcome from these meetings. Some people were blessed with the preaching of the Word of God. Others were haunted by the condemnation and judgment that they endured as they were arbitrarily singled out for humiliation or manipulation with guilt. Still others found their comfort in the hymns and special songs that were sung during the services. For those who came to seek God and Him alone, they were never disappointed. The quiet hickory grove was conducive to prayer and meditation. For that reason and that alone the name "Emmanuel" was always precious to Priscilla, no matter how ravished she felt by her shame or her guilt.

The only contact with the outside world during those ten days was the trip made into the nearest town to do the laundry. What fun it was to ride around in the wire laundry carts, use quarters to purchase the cute little boxes of Cheer and Downy and to come back to the campground with a fresh load of clothes! Equally delightful was to find another family friend at the laundromat, where the children had the rare opportunity to play together, briefly.

It was after this type of camp meeting when the Watkins returned home, not knowing that storm clouds were gathering. Frank got up to carry on the regular service that Sunday morning and stated that he was unable to preach because he did not know if he was still a Christian. He took a knee right then and there by the pulpit and began to pray. As he prayed, Mrs. South arose from her seat with her floral handkerchief and began to pace back and forth in front of the pulpit. As her hands rose so did her voice calling down rebuke upon the pastor bowed by the pulpit. As he humbly submitted to her usurpation of authority, something within Priscilla rose white-hot against the injustice. "That can't be right!" she thought. "I live with this man night and day and he has done nothing wrong." It would be twelve more years before she heard of the wonderful concept of God's sovereignty and how what Satan means for evil God can use for good.

"But as for you, ye thought evil against me; but God meant it unto good, to bring to pass, as it is this day, to save much people alive" (Genesis 50:20).

The Last Day

The brown house by the railroad track had another familiar rhythm, reminiscent of Flossie's tip-toeing black shoes across the girls' bedroom. It was the passenger train that ran every morning and evening and was always on time. Margaret was getting better, and her peace was returning after the comfort of scripture had been soaking into her soul along with the doctor's medications. Rest, and the support of family, were also helping her heal and Flossie had returned to her own home. She was no longer needed for daily housekeeping and parenting support.

Late in the summer an announcement was made in the Mahoning Message. The passenger line was being removed and would no longer be seen on the track. The girls crept to the window early one morning with Frank so they could see the last morning train. That evening, the final evening train passed the other direction and the end of an era quietly slid into oblivion as the caboose disappeared down the track.

Following the demise of the passenger train, another final day was coming of which the Watkins family was unaware. It was time for the annual meeting, which came around every late spring. During that time, the superintendent would come and meet with the church in the absence of the pastor and all would vote on whether or not he should stay.

The Watkins cowered downstairs under the stairway during the meeting. They were unsure of what the outcome would be. Hushed whispers between Margaret and Frank indicated to the girls that maybe everything was not going to be all right. The meeting was going longer than expected and the anxiety in Frank's eyes was mounting. Sweat beaded in his palms and Margaret nervously bit her lower lip. Calming the girls, she said, "We will know soon". Though they tried to be sympathetic out of loyalty to their parents, they secretly were terribly excited about the possibility that the Grey Elephant would be coming again soon.

A deliberate footfall on the stairs above signaled the meeting was over and Bro. Filbert was coming downstairs. Without a word and with superficial smiles all around, the family drove home with the attending superintendent, Brother Filbert, in the front seat beside Frank. The next morning Frank and Margaret broke the news to the girls. "We are moving in two weeks, but we don't know where."

Priscilla jumped out of her chair while it swung backward, bumping the monolithic antique sideboard without so much as a dent. Grabbing Bridget, they jumped up and down. It was a difficult time for Frank and Margaret but loads of fun for Bridget and Priscilla. They were delighted to spend a week with their cousin and cousin soon-to-be-born in southwestern Ohio. Frank was thankful for some time with his father over in West Virginia. In two weeks, a default plan of going west was in place and the family was packed and ready to move in the Grey Elephant once again. This time two different Bible school boys arrived to drive the moving truck. In late July, the Watkins turned their car west and traveled with the Grey Elephant, two college students and two wiggly girls in the back seat along the silver ribbon of Interstate 70. Of course, there was no air conditioning for the entire trip.

Mountain Skyline

The transition was hard. Frank was defeated, Margaret was humiliated and there was hardly a penny to spare for anything. The Whites, who pastored the large church of the Bible school in the west, offered their small trailer at the top of the hill by the cemetery as a home for the new family. Frank and Margaret were thankful for a place into which they could move. The next week, Frank went to work with a local painting contractor and when the recession of the seventies hit a few weeks later, he began "hod carrying" for a local plasterer which meant that he was up and down scaffolding all day long with a platter of mud to stucco the new housing. He would come home at night exhausted and immediately fall into a deep sleep on the living room floor, flat on his sore back.

Margaret began sewing for ladies in the church and Bible college. Since women only wore homemade dresses, the market was infinite. She labored hard on tailored outfits for $5.00 a dress. Wedding dresses, suits, trousseaus, aprons, veils, hats, slips, nightwear – all were subject to her nimble fingers. Bridget was the tallest in her class, extremely thin and very smart. She was disappointed because it was so hard to make friends. Priscilla, always able to go with the flow in the security of her parents' love, found each new event an adventure.

The family's rented trailer came with a chicken coop in the backyard. Priscilla was delighted at this new opportunity to observe and enjoy something she knew nothing about. She gathered the eggs for the Whites diligently and was devastated one morning when she broke two eggs as she picked them up out of the scratchy straw. All day she was frightened as she waited for Will to show up so she could confess her terrible sin. He was kind and smiled, telling her she was forgiven.

The sunsets were glorious over the bluff that hid Pikes Peak from the Watkins' trailer. The deep pinks and coral stripes with orange made each evening a surprise presentation, straight from the brush of God. Those were happy days, for home is where the heart is. Though Frank and Margaret were working very hard and the trailer was crowded and rather cold, all their needs were met, and they had each other. Many dark evenings were spent house-hunting after Frank got home from work. Margaret was just sure that they could find a house to buy that was affordable because she did not want to "throw money down a rat-hole" paying rent. It was a safe little community to live in because five of the surrounding houses were lived in by families who attended the church and school where the Watkins also went. Across the road in a huge field was The Tabernacle, a large, white, wooden structure in which yearly commencements and camp meetings were held in the spring and summer. With wooden theater seating and shavings on the floor, it was easy to maintain the building and a pleasant cross-breeze flowed through the open windows in the evening during the church services.

It was a sunny afternoon when Bridget and Priscilla rode their bikes the mile from school, walking them the final two blocks uphill to the trailer. Walking in the door they saw Margaret seated at the sewing machine in the sunroom. She had just placed some oil in a large pot on the stove to make Tater Tots for lunch. Little did she know that the oil was getting too hot and as she walked into the kitchen to finish lunch, the oil ignited and burst into flames. There was no back door off the kitchen, so she had to make it from the kitchen through the living room, around the corner to the sunroom and down the breezeway to the backdoor. By this time flames were leaping up her hands and wrist. She kept setting the pot down, but it kept starting a fire wherever she left it. Quickly she raced out the front screen door and placed the pot on the sidewalk while the girls attended to her wretched burns. Just then, Priscilla's leg began to sting, and she looked down to see the nylon, dotted-Swiss fabric that she was wearing was melting and sticking to her leg. By then, Miss Warner and Mrs. Guinn had arrived by the front door. They were neighbors and took Margaret to the doctor immediately to dress her 3rd degree burns with Butesin Picrate, a burn ointment. It was a long process of healing and the scars on Priscilla's leg never went away.

In December, the short three-month stay in the trailer was over and Frank and Margaret re-financed their car loan to obtain the down payment on a little white two-bedroom house on Twenty-fifth Street. Priscilla cried. The new house was smelly, dirty and scary, and she was afraid that it would burn down

85

because it had a pilot light in the stove. Priscilla watched in awe as her mother turned the grimy yellow stove into a gleaming white work of restored art.

Priscilla must have forgotten how her skilled father who could fix anything. Mr. Fix-It, Paint-It, Make-It-Work. The family moved from the trailer to the little house in early December and enjoyed having a place to call their own home for the first time in their lives. The back porch was walled with paned windows that spilled light into every corner. The kitchen was dreary and had a spruce green floor and a tiny countertop about a total of four cubic feet. The tiles on the floor and the curvaceous little fridge dated the kitchen to the late forties, at least. Hardwood floors with a swarthy patina surrounded the rugs in the front living room and parlor.

After living in the little house for a year and taking monthly mortgage payment checks in the amount of one hundred dollars to the owner on the way to and from school, the girls had a terrible fright. It was a dark winter night and their father had been working two jobs to provide for the family's needs. He worked during the day as a janitor for the wastewater division of the city. In the evening, he would paint or do household remodeling to make the ends of the paycheck meet. On one of those evenings, Frank was driving home from work, after ten o'clock in the evening, when he stopped at the intersection of a busy highway. Being a slow reactor, he hesitated a moment before turning left on the green arrow to cross the intersection. Suddenly, "Wham!" Speeding down the mountain pass at over one hundred miles per hour, a Chevrolet Caprice broadsided his blue Ford in the left, front fender. The car continued, hitting another vehicle in the opposite lane before u-turning, colliding with a light post, severing both the car and driver in two, and coming to a complete stop.

Priscilla's father was temporarily dazed and realized he had a lot of pain in his shoulder and rib cage. After being transported to the hospital by ambulance, he had no further injuries than a broken collarbone and two broken ribs. However, the concussion he sustained when his head struck the door post resulted in a lifelong challenge of restless-leg syndrome while he slept.

Being the compliant girls that Priscilla and Bridget were, they knew that once they were in bed they were never supposed to get up after bedtime, especially when it was a school night. So, when they heard their mother talking on the telephone and the quiet filtering in of family as uncles and aunts came to help them figure out why their father had not come home yet from work, they simply clung to each other and cried in fear.

The next few weeks brought an outpouring of love and encouragement on the struggling little family as they received food, gifts, visits and cards from their family and friends right before Christmas. Best of all was that their beloved father and provider had not been taken from them and was sitting in the living room alive and well but unable to laugh because of his broken ribs! Their mother often reminded them over the years of this unbelievable sparing of their father's life and showed them with great sadness when she received a little note of thanks from the nineteen-year-old, widowed mother and her infant son. Her compassion for the driver's family was greater than her anger or desire for justice to be served. Insurance soon provided another car but for years they would pull out the newspaper clipping of the totaled Ford and wonder at God's protective care.

The little back bedroom that sloped towards the

garage and chicken coop had two big windows graced with gauzy, white curtains. There was no closet, but an old metal wardrobe served the purpose. The girls' young cousin loaned them a handmade bookcase from her well-appointed bedroom. It had two shelves and two drawers. The fringe benefit of forced organization was learned quickly as they had to keep track of their clothes in a limited space. Bridget was unconcerned about the intricate details of color-coded handkerchiefs in an ironed stack, but Priscilla added that to her growing list of "ought-tos". In addition, she closely monitored the side of the bed upon which Bridget slept and made sure she did not cross the imaginary line. Priscilla was heading into a phase of downright snitty criticism for her good sister and made use of every opportunity to display it. When they made their double bed together in the morning before school, Priscilla would watch closely to see what she could point out as being wrong. With glee she would leave her side of the bed impeccable and with a miffed attitude stalk out of the bedroom to walk to school, holding her head high as she walked along with Bridget. With legalism often comes arrogance because a list of do's and don'ts is so easy to flaunt.

True virtue is not so easy to measure.

One day the girls went shopping after school with their parents. Margaret had decided that it was time to upgrade the girls' sleeping situation. She deliberately purchased two matching, pink, box spring and mattress sets along with Hollywood frames. They were delivered to the little house a few days later. Within a day, Margaret had shopped for, designed and made matching blue bedspreads with seams down the edge of each spread. They were soft, light and beautiful. Though there was no door on their new room, the girls were thrilled to switch bedrooms with their parents and have their own beds in the tiny room between the kitchen and bathroom.

A stray kitten made its way to their door and to the delight of the girls, their parents said they could adopt it. Times were difficult and the milk that Margaret made for the girls was out of a large, Carnation, powered-milk container. However, it was even more diluted with water to make it stretch. This is all that was being fed to the kitty and it did not survive. The neighbors gently told Margaret that they had found it under a bush because it had passed away from hunger. Margaret was sorry that times were so hard that the kitten had died because she did not know any better.

During these years Priscilla began to often get sick. Nothing serious, but every little virus going around always seemed to get her down. Bridget could be exposed to an identical bug, spike a fever and be terribly ill for a day but back in school the next day. Priscilla would languish at home half sick and half well, irritable but happy to follow her mother from sewing to ironing with her makeshift bed of two kitchen chairs, padded by a pillow and quilt. She would often be struggling with sore throats and colds and right after her eighth-grade graduation, it was a relief to have a tonsillectomy and get rid of the pain and missed days of school.

Though the bathroom was primitive with its old fixtures including a claw foot tub, Margaret decorated it in style. The walls were painted a fresh, light green. She made jaunty curtains for the window and coordinated the toilet seat cover with the double-knit scraps from some of her dresses she had made. It had a beautiful white daisy appliquéd on top. When Sarah came to visit, she said, "This room is so beautiful you could have your devotions in here." Next to the bathroom was a huge walk-in closet that Margaret fashioned with a curtain for privacy.

The most exciting transformation of all was the kitchen makeover. Frank lowered the ceiling, painted the cabinets a creamy white and put in a new countertop. As he tore apart the old walls, he found a fascinating piece of insulation: an old newspaper dated 1902. He added a new sink and refrigerator and put in a new floor with golden-patterned tile. During the decorating phase, Margaret had a bright idea. "Let's decorate the inset of the cupboard doors on the bias!" she said exuberantly.

"I don't know what you mean, Margaret," returned Frank with a puzzled look. Grabbing the wallpaper and her scissors, Margaret held the plaid wallpaper up to the cupboard door at an angle with the plaid on its' side like lattice.

"See? This is what it would look like. And I'll match the plaid while I cut it out." They went to work on their project and in a few hours the cupboards looked darling. Frank had removed all the little green, depression-glass handles to clean them with mineral spirits, and now he returned them to the doors and drawers where they belonged. The whole kitchen looked fetching with this little improvement in the tiny baking and cooking corner. It was on that very countertop that Priscilla woke up one morning to see a paper lying with important news. "Cease Fire!" The long Vietnam War had come to an end.

The next summer a major landscaping project began in the front yard. Frank graded the lawn by hand and improved the drainage problems of the winter by building forms for a tiny retaining wall. He ripped out the old sidewalk at the same time and prepared a nice walkway to the front of the house. Fresh sod was placed throughout the front yard making his wife and daughters skip for joy. The bushes were trimmed back, and the yellow roses bloomed prolifically that year. Though it seemed that the leadership of the church was bowed down to and honored in an unhealthy way, still the unpopular little family felt very honored when their yellow roses were selected for the fiftieth wedding anniversary celebration of the senior leader of the Emmanuel Association of Churches. His nieces came and picked a bouquet themselves because the roses were like what he picked for her when they were dating. A mock orange tree scented the side of the house along with some lilacs, and Bridget and

Priscilla enjoyed clipping a sprig of the mock orange and placing it in their hair pretending to be brides on their wedding day. Margaret had told them it was a traditional wedding flower.

Money was very tight and there was not enough to landscape the backyard at that time. No matter, the backyard had its own quirky charm with a chicken coop and old garage. Big apple trees provided shade and fun places to climb. A clothesline helped Margaret conserve energy as she hung out the freshly washed clothes, teaching the girls how to hang the items all together with the undies on the inside and the sheets and dresses on the outside of the lines. When the work was done, there was always time to play out in the chicken coop! There were three separate shacks in a row and each girl had moved into her own "house". When a friend came over to play, there was an extra coop for her. No chickens were in the chicken house now, but there were reminders of their recent occupation of the setting area. It was covered with a slanted wooden door much like a chest freezer, or so the girls thought, and they made a point out of placing the washed containers of diminutive sizes such as ice cream or salt in their imaginary "freezer". Cast off rugs, chairs, or lamps from relatives increased their quality of life in the chicken coop. And still their wealthy little friends sang its praises!

It was in this alley, between the preset boundaries of the fence post and the neighbors' property, that Priscilla rode her bike, up and down, day after day, but with her imagination, it was anything but monotonous. The entire time was spent composing stories in her head of how she would help impoverished children someday. She loved biographies such as "The Little Woman", "Walking with Jesus", "Little Tiny of Nigeria", and the stories of Florence Nightingale, Jane Addams and Catherine Booth. Her own parents' compassion for those in need fueled her desire. All she could imagine in her future was a post somewhere in the world where God would place her with the responsibility of caring for needy children, telling them about their Creator and His great love and purpose for their lives. To that end, she imagined, prayed, dreamed, hoped and wrote endless stories in her thoughts as she played.

One day, Priscilla went out to ride her bike and it was gone. Not yet had the sophistication of a bike lock or a storage area in the garage come to their minds, and the bikes were always leaned alongside the house. Since her daddy was painting with a friend in another neighborhood, he told him about what had happened. Curiously, they found her bike leaning against a tree at another person's home nearby and came home to make a sign. It read, "We came to take our bike back. If you need to borrow it again, please ask the next time." He took the bike back and returned it home to her that evening.

Under the tree by the back door where the milk box stood, the girls arranged a small rock garden. It had hen and chickens, periwinkle, moss rose and a collection of rocks from the mountains. Feeling a great need to create another "park", Bridget and Priscilla got an old turquoise enamel roaster and dug a hole just its size in the middle of the garden. They placed a pretty rock in the side of the oval "pond" and filled it with water. How special they would feel as they sat and daydreamed while they gazed into their tiny pool! Every child needs a special place to think and dream.

School was going to be starting soon and Margaret had always made the girls three new dresses every fall. This time however, she was very busy and decided it was time to help the girls learn to sew their own clothes. After a fun trip to the fabric store, Mill Outlet, she purchased some fabric and brought it home. With her help, they cut out their own dresses from her simple, homemade patterns. She could just look at the armholes and side seams and adjust them every year for her growing children. With some fitting along the way as the sewing was done, they always looked custom-designed and the girls were as neat as a pin. Priscilla sat on the sun porch many afternoons that summer at ten years of age, pinning and re-pinning her zipper while her hands dripped with sweat from the anxiety of doing something that she did not feel confident about but was sure had to be perfect when it was done. The fabric was practically thread-bare from ripping when her dress was complete, but at least she had started and would never turn back. For some reason it was Bridget who was finally able to explain to her how to fold the fabric just so around the nubbin of the zipper and make it all look hidden on purpose.

Bridget was accustomed to patience-producing work in solitude. Her fingers were nimble, and her hands did not sweat. She could see the big picture of the project while she worked. She also had a talent for transferring knowledge from one project to another and soon was stitching up doll clothes and doing intricate embroidery.

Music Notes

The girls began taking piano lessons. Back in Newton Falls when Margaret was so ill, Frank had taken her shopping one winter evening for a brand-new piano. The girls tagged along on many piano-shopping trips after that. They were afraid they would never be able to enter a piano store again. However, they learned all the differences between major brand names such as Steinway, Sohmer, Kimball, Baldwin and all the nuances of each. Margaret would test each piano and came back to an elegant walnut-finished Sohmer with a beautiful music rest that included gold lattice and a carved cameo in the center.

The perfect piano was delivered to the big house in Ohio and became a family treasure from that day forward. The piano was always treated with great respect. No pencil was allowed on the surface. Little hands were supposed to stay on the keys so as not to scratch the back of the keys with their fingernails or leave fingerprints on the gleaming wood. A book was never supposed to be scooted across the top of the piano in case a piece of dust would scratch the surface. And God pity the aunt who would make the mistake of placing her three-ring binder on the music rack while practicing for a special song in church. The dimple left in the soft wood from her notebook brought a gasp from a distraught Margaret. For the piano bench, Margaret tailored a cover, which included perfectly proportioned box pleats and fabric-covered cording in a pattern to compliment the living room furniture.

Bridget and Priscilla were both enrolled in piano lessons at the Bible school, Emmanuel Academy, where they attended. They enjoyed their teachers and practiced thirty minutes every day. Often Priscilla would burst in from school and sit down at the piano to practice. A few minutes later she would be bent over the keyboard crying because she did not know how long she had practiced. She had to be perfectly honest about her reporting and was unable to do so without starting all over again. Such fear stemmed from the guilt she would have if she lied about even one minute. She must have an accurate record, because lying would certainly place her on the path to hell. Margaret kept the home going with the help of her kitchen timer and used it for piano practice as well. She had excellent musical ability and was a piano teacher with lots of experience. She had a high standard for the girls and Priscilla felt like she never measured up to her mother's expectations.

School included a typical elementary curriculum with chapel every morning and opening exercises every afternoon. These times included singing, prayer and scripture study along with a character-building book read out loud to the children. Best of all, during these times, were the scripture memory opportunities that helped the children hide God's word in their hearts, never to forget it. There were many techniques, but a favorite was the alphabetical system where every week a verse was written across the top of the chalkboard in the teacher's perfect cursive. The verses always began with the letter of the alphabet that they were ready for that week. For example, "A good name is rather to be chosen than great riches and loving favor rather than silver and gold" (Proverbs 22:1). Or "Be ye kind one to another, tenderhearted, forgiving one another, even as God for Christ's sake has forgiven you" (Ephesians 4:22). These, and the many years of other verses that followed them, stayed in the children's hearts and came back to comfort and encourage them in the hard times that lay ahead.

In the classrooms, the teachers insisted upon a high standard of decorum. Children walked in a quiet line with their hands behind their backs when passing from class to chapel, recess, the restrooms and lunch. In class, no one ever thought of whispering to each other and even smiles were disciplined at times. Everyone always faced the front of the class. Priscilla was a very particular young lady with strong feelings about clean hands. When the boys would visit the restrooms, sometimes they would return to the waiting line so quickly that the toilet could be heard flushing as they opened the door. Priscilla would cringe if that same boy touched a ball that she had to touch, knowing that he had not washed his hands. It was uncomfortable to the point of making her feel anguished. And woe unto the young man who touched her book when returning from that restroom if he had not washed his hands either. Sometimes the boys were spunky and would grab a wandering pigtail and pin it to the desk with a pencil. When the unaware girl would get out of her seat, a mild whiplash was sure to follow.

During these elementary years Priscilla had a challenging trial that was used to develop character in her though it hurt deeply. In her second semester of fourth grade, the teacher chose to not return to finish the school year and her aunt took over the classroom instead. It seemed that Aunt Joan had a specific conviction that Priscilla was too carefree and needed to be humbled and reminded of how inferior she was to her sister. She made a point of reminding Priscilla of her sister's competence over her own and took any opportunity to shame her in front of the class. It was not long before Aunt Joan's mother, Priscilla's grandmother, developed the same attitude and would ask Priscilla to move so Bridget could sit beside her at family visits. Even though Aunt Joan was a family member, Priscilla's mother was extremely wise with her daughters during this time. She would pray with Priscilla every day when she came home for lunch and ask God to help her be strong and respectful that afternoon. She did not belittle Bridget nor take matters into her own hands for resolution. She hugged Priscilla and listened to the tearful stories of humiliation that she recounted day after day. Though Priscilla was often comforted, she constantly internalized the message that she was not intelligent and would never be as successful as her sister. Given this presumed opinion, she still admired her sister, Bridget, knowing it was not her responsibility that the teacher chose to show favoritism between the two girls. Bridget became accustomed to the smell of the Campho Phenique solution that Aunt Joan placed on her constant canker sores and at times wondered if maybe teaching was not something that Aunt Joan enjoyed. She always seemed so unhappy while she was in the classroom.

A delightful gift was waiting at the end of elementary school in the seventh and eighth grades with Miss Springfield, a jolly, confident teacher who was tall, endowed and wore her thick brown hair in a figure-eight bun at the top of her neck. She had a warm, engaging smile, a tried-and true teaching style and curriculum and a joyful confidence that completed her personality for the job. She had no favorites, loved teaching, loved her students, REALLY loved Jesus and always loved life. She had an old Bible that she kept upright in the books on her desk and read a selection of Proverbs from it every single day for the two years each child was in her class. It was amazing how appropriate those wisdom scriptures were in the life of the students and how much of it they remembered for the rest of their lives. Every day she would mark where she quit reading with her red pencil and pick up where she left off the next morning. This gift was invaluable for these growing children.

State history was an important part of the curriculum. Each child made a lovely wooden, balsam scrapbook in the shape of Colorado with the rivers and towns intricately burned into the surface of the book. It was sanded, varnished and tied at the left with a leather shoestring. The pages inside included reports of Spanish explorers, collections of data about the natural history of the state and pictures of the state bird and flower with details about gold mining. These books and the Bible scrolls stood out as the favorite keepsakes of every student.

The Bible scrolls were twelve-inch tall strips of newsprint wound on wooden dowels with fancy finials at the top and bottom of each dowel. The scrolls were neatly wound around each dowel and starting in Genesis, a pictorial history of the entire Bible was drawn on newsprint by each student during Bible class every day. The ark, children of

Israel wandering in the wilderness and the cross of Calvary were high points that were not only intriguing to draw but visually impacted the faith of the children as they followed a "blood line" throughout the entire scroll. It was a narrow ribbon of red crayon that showed God's covenant promise long before Priscilla had ever heard of that brand of theology, as it was explained to her later in college. The "blood line" began in the Garden of Eden when Adam and Eve sinned, and God's plan of redemption began in the prophesy that their seed would crush Satan's head.

"And I will put enmity between thee and the woman, and between thy seed and her seed; it shall bruise thy head, and thou shalt bruise his heel" (Genesis 3:15).

The eighth-grade graduation day was much anticipated. The younger students looked up to them and anticipated the day when they would be the one starring on Graduation Day. Miss Springfield called the students into a special meeting to give them an opportunity to plan for their motto, usually built upon a scripture verse. They chose class colors and each student was assigned a special production such as a memorized "reading" or a piano solo. All was a secret and on a day towards the end of the year, the entire graduating class of two to three students would descend the hill to Potter Park where they would have cake and ice cream and give the teacher a gift. Priscilla and Andrew graduated together with the colors blue and yellow. The motto was "Jesus, the Master Builder" from the scripture verse, "According to the grace of God which is given unto me, as a wise masterbuilder, I have laid the foundation, and another buildeth thereon. But let every man take heed how he buildeth thereupon" (1 Corinthians 3:10). Priscilla's mother made her a new dress, a little longer than usual as she was growing up and would begin to wear her dresses ten inches from the floor now instead of just below the knee. In addition, this was the summer when Priscilla would experiment with new hairstyles that ranged from differing partings on one side or the other and a slightly less tight pulling of her hair back into braids. She would be switching from brown stockings to black in the fall marking another important milestone of maturity. Then there was the change from brown to black shoes, still with at least six eyelets to be sure that the foot was completely covered and modest. Brown shoes could never be worn after eighth grade.

Priscilla was so excited to be growing up. She watched the older girls in high school come and go to church and copied every move. How they folded their handkerchief just so on top of their Bible and walked into the church quietly, kneeling by the pew to pray before the service. How they sat with one hand delicately arranged on one cheek. Especially the way the big girls combed their hair and who looked the neatest of all. She also was intrigued by the dark, shadowy creatures who sat on the other side of the aisle at church. They were referred to as boys and wore dark pants, shoes and socks with dark golf jackets over button down shirts. It was completely illegal to look at any of them in their seats during school or church. Even worse was to look one in the eye for more than a brief "Good morning" if they happened to pass on the sidewalk while walking with their father or mother. Since Priscilla and Bridget had no brothers, they were completely unaware of how the other side of the world lived, namely the boys. They would not watch them and did not talk to them and kept all the social rules to the last detail of the law. However, such restraint did little for the matters of the heart that ranged from a light crush to a full blown smitten, distracted state of mind. These feelings were intensified by the secretive nature of young love and the enormity grew in Priscilla's imaginative mind because she was not supposed to discuss it with anyone other than her mother. And secrets can get awfully big!

Hearts and Flowers

One immeasurable blessing for Bridget and Priscilla was their mother's understanding of friendship. She was a good friend to others and called into question the wisdom of the old rule that mothers should not befriend their daughters. Though she never lost her authority as a parent, she was a good friend, confidant and listener to their heart secrets. Her desire for their purity brought her to her knees many times but it also kept her as a caring friend and the first person with whom they would share their questions and burdens.

Priscilla continued to mature and in preparation for high school was collecting the changing pieces for her grown-up wardrobe. Lots of brown and navy and dark green colored the closet and she now had a stash of silky, gunmetal-colored, seamed hose from Hibbards' in her dresser drawer. These were the only stockings the girls could wear, and they were purchased from an ancient department store downtown. Entering it made you feel like you were going to a museum with the old board floors, glass and wooden display cabinets and unique accounting system. The ladies at the various departments would take the payment; place it in a tiny canister like a bank teller window carrier. "Whoosh!" Away it would go in the clear pipes of the store, back to the accounting office for either the change and receipt or the crediting to the shopper's account. In the four-floor department store there was also a vintage elevator with a movable, metal, lattice door inside where a lady sat on a wooden bar stool and operated it for all the customers. It was at this store that the prescribed stockings were purchased and came in their own perfect pink and yellow gift box with tissue on the inside. Handkerchiefs were also available in the display case across the aisle and were the perfect birthday or graduation gift for a friend. Each handkerchief also came in its own gift box, if requested, and was perfectly starched, folded and looked elegant with delicate floral embroidery and lace around the edges. Priscilla often wondered what year these fashions dated back towards because she did not see other girls her age riding their bicycles along the busy avenue in black-seamed silken hosiery and full skirts. But it seemed best not to ask questions about that topic, because it may result in a later altar confession at a future church service.

About this time the girls began band and chorus in their freshman and sophomore years of high school. There were many opportunities for music at the private high school that met in the buildings around the church where their parents had married. Across the street there was a self-standing publishing office and print shop which was vital in distributing the needed literature across the Emmanuel Circle of Churches in order to keep standardized lifestyles and cultural mores. It was an immaculate building with a classroom on one side and the other wing held a band room and individual music studios, which had a piano in each one. Some instruments such as the tuba, drums and marimba were the property of the school, but most students provided their own. Mr. and Mrs. Watkins were careful to help their daughters select the instrument that they both desired. Bridget chose the trumpet and Priscila wanted to be like her mother and play the alto saxophone. Her instrument was silver with a gold bell and came in a grey case lined with blue velvet. With several years of lessons, she was soon ready to play in the band with all the other students. How fun this was, both as a musical outlet but also as a social opportunity. For once they could sit beside a friend and possibly talk to them, at least about the music. Sacred arrangements and ensembles were played for church services, in addition to other standard band pieces such as Sousa's marches and Viennese waltzes. Every Christmas and spring there would be a program prepared for the church people and some from the community would come as well.

A gifted science teacher introduced Priscilla to biology when she was a freshman in high school. Still spending many days too sick to go to school, her sister and the teacher devised a way for Priscilla's education to continue at home in the area of anatomy. At the science lab, the class was dissecting a fetal pig, and though the smell of formaldehyde was overwhelming, it also came in handy for their plan. Placing said piglet in a plastic grocery bag, Brigette pedaled home from school on her bike and placed it carefully in the bathtub to tutor Little Sis with the learnings of the day. Said piglet was stored in the cold car overnight only to be returned by bicycle the following day in order to continue biology lab.

Priscilla loved the chorus practice nights the most of all. She was thrilled to sit beside her cousin who was like a brother to her. He was one year older and sang bass while she sang alto. Boys and girls never sat beside each other unless they were cousins or brother and sister. On occasion there would be two who played a trumpet and did "have" to sit beside each other, but the strictest decorum abided in their conversation and demeanor. Though it was hard for Priscilla to admit it at the time, she was starting to feel differently about one boy particularly. He was tall and had dark hair just like her beloved daddy, and because he had not grown up locally, he was mysterious. He had a notable hunger for God and that made him even more attractive to her. She could not understand why she got so distracted when he was in the room or sat with his family on her side of the church. She was only thirteen and she was sure she was too young to even think about such things.

With the beginning of high school came a delightful upgrade to Priscilla's own bedroom. In the past years her family had moved from the simple old white house that her father remodeled to a lovely stucco home at the base of Garden of the Gods. Once again, it was scary at first to go through all that change. The house was not yet home, and though better, it did not smell right. It had not yet had the touch of her father's paintbrush nor the fury of her mother's scrubbing brush. The new neighborhood was called Pleasant Valley and that it was.

A creative gardener had landscaped the home previously and there were spruce, plum and ash trees, junipers, bridal wreath, lilacs, ash trees, roses, four-o'clocks, hot pokers and many other perennial flowers. A perfectly fenced yard made it possible for the girls to dream of truly owning a dog safely and they had three consecutive Huskies: Tonuk, Inatuk and Blizzard, over the next thirteen years. The new property offered yet another landscape for their father's carpentry skills. He created a beautiful deck at the back of the house and built a two-car garage, with room along the side for his wood-working tools, to create projects in his spare time. It was also his private prayer room where he would spend time walking back and forth in the garage talking to his heavenly Father.

Across the street from the home in Pleasant Valley were horse stables and a sloping pasture backed up against the foothills. A gentle stream ran through the pasture. The horses provided constant entertainment for the girls or their friends when they would go over to visit. They loved to stroke the large cheeks of the huge animals, watching them constantly flicking the flies away with their tails. Horseshoeing was interesting to watch as well.

There were many people on the west side of town who attended the churches' main headquarters and some of them taught at the school as well. One of those was the algebra teacher who ambitiously decided to move a large two-story home from a historic street onto the hillside around the corner from their home in Pleasant Valley. He brought it across town slowly on a huge trailer, set it on the foundation he had already built, remodeled and painted it a lovely yellow and there it stood, with a grand view of the valley.

For the Watkins family, there was a happy surprise building in the neighbor's home to the north of them. Four young men moved into a house in need of repairs and they all started fixing it up, landscaping, involving themselves in grass-roots politics and gently reaching out in friendship to the fearful neighbors to the south. Frank told Margaret, "One of these days, one of those boys is going to fall in love and kick the other three out." Soon it happened. Dave and Linsey were engaged and invited the Watkins family to their wedding at the beautiful Glen Eyrie Castle. It was a magical day and the joy of the young couple, the beauty of the surroundings and the evident blessing of Christ on their marriage was inspiring to all. A few months later, Linsey invited Margaret and the girls over for lunch one afternoon. It was such a tasty lunch of sandwiches and Doritos, but most memorable was the spirit that was served up at the table and permeated her home. In this simple act of kindness, a ray of hope penetrated a dark and fearful faith that needed to be set free.

For Priscilla's graduation she had received gifts of money and purchased a dark-wood canopy bed and dresser. It was fun to express herself a little bit with a soft pink bedspread. Her room was becoming a haven for both joy and sorrow as she continued to grow. It was a sweet conglomerate of dolls, books, papers and lots of questions. Questions about life's suffering. Love. Family relationships. Health. Haves and have-nots. Shoulds and should-nots. A place for dreams and nightmares. It was a place to cry, to pray, to read, to try to study and a place to practice her saxophone. But still, it was a haven and a place to grow. And a place to sleep the last night before her wedding day, thankful for the protection and peace her parents provided for twenty-six years.

Priscilla spent many nights falling asleep with sadness, longing for the dream of that hoped-for phantom of love, yet dreading that it may be happening to her already and praying that it was not! Nothing this powerful had ever taken over her and she did not know what to do with it for sure. A steady mother was her rock during much of the time until church tremors of an upcoming earthquake shook her foundations.

Part III

Pursuit for Truth

Turning Point

Though a time of polarized joy and fear, high school provided tremendous growth in Priscilla. Her sophomore year of high school was over, and she started to work more outside the home that summer. She cleaned houses with her sister and others who were old enough to drive her to their jobs, and she spent some great times with her cousins. It was also the time to open savings accounts and contribute their earnings towards tithe, education and ice cream impulses. Trips to the mountains for cabin vacations with her sister and parents added to her memory bank of happiness.

One afternoon her father was driving across town and Priscilla was in the back seat.

"Daddy, do I really have to read the Bible every day?" she asked.

"Yes," her father slowly answered. "You should at least try to do so."

"Do I have to read a whole chapter?" she asked.

"Yes, you should," was his reply.

Obediently but reluctantly, Priscilla started reading in the book of John. One evening she read the words: "Hitherto have ye asked nothing in my name: ask, and ye shall receive, that your joy may be full" (John 16:24). Priscilla was amazed that this verse resonated with her. She could not forget it, either. Realizing that her joy was certainly not full, she kept reading, partly out of curiosity and partly because she wanted to obey her father.

Priscilla's independent heart that summer was challenged inside where no one could see. She did not respect her mother and did not even really like her. In her irritable disposition she was constantly being agitated and finding fault with her family. Though she apologized to her mother, she had no power to change herself. She continued to read her Bible with drudgery and found sitting through the worship with hymns at church completely boring.

She was almost fourteen the August that the western camp meeting was held on the south end of town. Priscilla went to church with her father alone one night when the evangelist preached from Ephesians 2:8-9. "For by grace are ye saved through faith; and that not of yourselves: it is the gift of God:

Not of works, lest any man should boast." Priscilla had heard the verse before, but never had it impacted her like that night. The elderly preacher earnestly illustrated what it was like to be "afar off" like the Israelites had been in the wilderness but "brought nigh [near]" by the blood of Jesus Christ, offered on the cross of Calvary for sin. It was the gospel, plain and clear, with no add-ons or plug-ins! The Holy Spirit of God Himself drew Priscilla's heart after Him, because no other way can a person come to the Heavenly Father. "Jesus saith unto him, I am the way, the truth, and the life: no man cometh unto the Father, but by me" (John 14:6). Drawn by His irresistible grace, Priscilla responded at the end of the sermon when the preacher invited seekers to come to the front of the old tabernacle with its wooden theatre seating, bark shavings for a floor and a wooden altar. There she knelt on the right side with the women while the men knelt on the left. She prayed and asked God to come "clear in". She wanted him to enter her heart because she believed in His gift of salvation that was not of works; clearly, she had plenty of time to have practiced that in the past thirteen years.

Her heart filled with inexpressible joy. She

knew she was a child of God! She bravely stood to her feet at the next pause in the prayer meeting and quietly stated that she knew she was saved. There was great rejoicing in heaven because this child had repented and accepted His salvation. Her daddy drove her home without any discussion, but when she got there, she rushed to her mother's bedroom to tell her the news. That night she kept waking up with joy and at one point just had to get out of bed and kneel there to thank Jesus for saving her from her sin.

The next day was another ordinary day of camp meeting, but Priscilla was different! This time she could not keep the smile from her face. The afternoon service began with a song from the paperback song books and Priscilla thought her heart would explode as they sang the words by William Ralph Featherston:

"*My Jesus, I love Thee, I know Thou art mine.*
For Thee All the follies of sin I resign.
My gracious Redeemer, My Savior art thou,
If ever I loved Thee, Lord Jesus 'tis now."

When she read the next chapter in her Bible as she had been doing that summer, the words nearly leaped off the page with meaning. Her soul had been ignited with a fire never to go out. It may smolder over the years, it may at times burst into flame, but the spark would never die.

Sadly, she did not know that the last part was true.

Part IV

Ethnocentricity Begins to Crumble

Fault Lines, Fissures and Other Rocky Mountain Moments

Priscilla's sophomore and junior years of high school were by far more magical than all the others. She was excited about each year, her classes and her teachers. The first year of high school had been tough. After starting first grade when her age was more suited to a kindergarten class, that little stretch of time in her developmental maturity finally caught up with her. The geometry and biology offered her freshman year were difficult; so difficult that she often compared herself with her older sister and cousin and despaired of ever fully understanding the difficult concepts she worked on every night. In addition, she was sick a lot and missed many days of school. Her parents decided on a tonsillectomy which made a big difference in reducing the number of infections.

Unfortunately, so small an academy did not offer a lot of room for variance and classes were only offered every other year to accommodate the small faculty and student body. In addition, there were family members in leadership who sometimes made biased decisions about what the students could study. Because of this, Priscilla was denied an opportunity to take algebra because she was advised she would probably not do as well as her sister. At the time it really didn't matter, because in such an insular world she never expected to need to understand or practice it. The same was true of chemistry. The limited boundaries of her culture made it too easy to compare each other among themselves and this is never wise.

"For we dare not make ourselves of the number, or compare ourselves with some that commend themselves: but they measuring themselves by themselves, and comparing themselves among themselves, are not wise" (2 Corinthians 10:12).

The brightest spot for Priscilla was her English teacher who honored every student equally and was sensitive to all. Priscilla was exposed to English and American literature and finally had an opportunity to study creative writing and get credit for coursework she adored. Not only that, she was good at writing and the teacher praised her work.

In her junior year the circle widened and more students from the outlying Circle of Churches were coming in to school from across the country. With them came more creative talent, and the poetry, essays and artwork captured from the small group of students that year was legendary.

Students continued to study Latin, English, history, science, typing, bookkeeping and loved the arts of music, writing and drawing in a variety of mediums. Sports were a difficult part of the curriculum due to several factors. The standards of apparel prohibited anything that could not be done in long pants and button-down shirts for the boys and dresses for the girls. Consequently, volleyball and baseball were the only actual ball games played.

No family owned a television or radio and many radios in vehicles were removed to comply with the church standards. It was forbidden to read the sports section of the newspaper, so competition of any type would not influence the students. However, this did not diminish the rousing games of volleyball played in long dresses that were especially fun on late summer evenings or spring school trips. It also provided a rare opportunity to socialize as boys and girls together unless the teams were separated by gender, which was sometimes the case.

With the Rocky Mountains as their backyard, geology and astronomy were especially thrilling subjects and even botany had its own allure, the arid desert notwithstanding. School trips up into the mountains were usually an entire day in length and included hiking, boating or ice skating, depending on the weather, picnicking and lots of photography. There were fault lines within a five-mile radius of their home that intrigued Priscilla. She would look at that massive upturned strata of granite rock and her father would point to her with his finger showing how the line of the earth's surface continued uninterrupted and then drastically dropped, continuing deep below. He explained that this was called a "fault line" that was close to the epicenter geologically noted in the southwestern county. Historically, there had been an earthquake there and could be again. Nearby, in a town at the foot of the mountains, were many mineral springs. One even had a beautiful concrete statute of a Ute Indian, bent over with his water jug where the spring water constantly flowed from his jug. A favorite treat on a hot summer evening was to head up to the "old Indian" with some plastic water jugs and collect the fresh spring water. It had a tangy bite to it, similar to carbonation. Priscilla's family would mix it with a package of Kool Aid and serve it over ice, making a simple yet happy memory.

For a girl who was afraid of the dark, the Russians, flooding, rape, the rapture, and now an earthquake, the fault line did not come as good news. The adults who realized how motivating towards good behavior these tactics could be sometimes abused the information. Armed with these facts, Priscilla had something new to fear, but also held it in great wonder and awe at the same time.

Not far from that fault line, another epicenter was starting to send faint tremors throughout the neighborhood. School was ending in the spring of the year and Bridget was getting ready to graduate from high school with a small, balanced group of friends. All the traditions were identical to those of their parents. The navy dress with the white collar for the graduation picture. An eight-by-ten, group photograph, with neat calligraphy of the graduates' names and year, was distributed to everyone.

There were junior and senior meetings as the class chose a president, vice president, secretary and treasurer. In Priscilla's junior class there were only three students, so they skipped the office of vice president. Plans were being made for the junior-senior reception, the spring music recital and the graduation at the end of May. No need for college planning or test scores; the graduates had only one option: return the following year and continue in the college that operated out of the base of the church on the Bible school's campus. It may have seemed simple compared to their current high school culture, but the anticipation on the part of the young people was no different. Priscilla admired her big sister for her intellect, musical and artistic ability and spiritual growth. Bridget was developing into a strong young lady and Priscilla had no other ambition than to follow in her steps. It was fun planning the details of the reception and keeping them a secret from her big sister. One night was devoted to cutting ice cream into individual servings of rectangular blocks, decorating them with icing and then refreezing them in preparation for the big night.

With class colors of purple and yellow and lilacs blooming all around the town, it was easy to decorate for the events. Yellow iris accented the bouquets of lilacs and all preparations were complete. The graduation was held in the very church where Margaret and Frank had graduated twenty-six years before. Bridget looked happy in her white graduation dress her mother had made and her white stockings and shoes. She wore a corsage but no graduation gown or mortarboard. A hand-designed diploma was handed out that looked identical to the ones her parents had received. Everything seemed to be going well. Priscilla and Bridget had registered for their ongoing classes that fall before all the students separated for the summer.

After many years of faithful employment at the city department of wastewater, Frank had a lot of vacation saved up and the family decided to go east for two weeks to visit Frank's family and attend the scheduled camp meeting in Kentucky that July.

Grandma and Grandpa Watkins were preparing for the vacation as well and reserved a lovely lodge in the Appalachian Mountains for the week. They bought a new Coleman cooler for the little family that was coming from the west. Grandpa Watkins was excellent at laying in provisions and he had watermelon on ice, sodas, sweets of all kinds and had reserved a final trip to the store for when the girls arrived just to select their favorite ice cream.

It was one of the best trips home that the family had ever experienced. There was lots of love and conversation, beautiful nature to enjoy, perfect weather and a mature appreciation for the gift of family. Frank had some heart-to-heart talks on the porch with his father about the church that they had been in for so many years. Mr. Watkins respected his son's decisions but felt uneasy about the closed atmosphere in which he watched him raising his family. Frank firmly promised his father that afternoon on the porch of the lodge that he would never leave the Emmanuel Circle of Churches. Priscilla witnessed it through the cabin windows.

Later, in the camp meeting that followed in Kentucky, Frank and Margaret noticed a difference in the teaching that was occurring over the pulpit in the wooden tabernacle. It seemed more centered on the Bible than what they were becoming used to in the west. They remarked on the difference to each other but did not discuss it in front of the children. However, on the way home from Kentucky that summer, Margaret started to get fragile emotionally again and several times in the muggy Ozarks, the family was not sure they would all make it home safe and sound. Memories of her prior psychotic episodes and the mental hospital had not been erased though it had been ten years since the last hospitalization. By the time everyone the family returned home, tension was building. The fault-line was shifting, and tremors were reverberating across the community. A full-fledged church split was in motion and by September, when the decisions of the academic calendar forced parents to take sides, Frank boldly made a visit to the pastor alone but with the support of his wife, Margaret. He visited him in his home and simply stated his concern that the preaching was not following Biblical proclamation of the gospel and because of that, the Watkins family would not be returning their children to school that fall. He further stated that he could not conscientiously attend church there anymore either but had no idea what the future would hold.

Such courage left the family shattered that next weekend. Wednesday had been their last night in church, yet they had not known it. Things happened rapidly and had a domino effect as the decisions were being made. Frank was wiped out from the conversation with the pastor. It would have been so much easier to gossip with others and sneak away with no explanation, but he took the biblical road of direct communication, outlined in Matthew eighteen, and spoke with his pastor instead.

"Moreover if thy brother shall trespass against thee, go and tell him his fault between thee and him alone: if he shall hear thee, thou hast gained thy brother" (Matthew 18:15).

Frank was exhausted by this action and his introvertive personality placed him in bed the following day, unable to even go to work. Margaret sat on the edge of their bed and asked Frank if he knew what he was going to do for the girls' education that fall. He responded that he had no idea.

Margaret's health continued to decline, and she had already been hospitalized in early August. Her behaviors changed in response to the incredible stress. Anxiety and depression clouded her face and she would sit rocking in the LazyBoy in the living room for hours, staring straight ahead. Then it would be time to go to bed and night after night she would be unable to sleep. Some of those nights she would just come into the living room and rock. Other times she would turn on all the lights and wake everyone else up because it was not fair for anyone else to sleep if she could not. One night, in her desperation, she called 9-1-1 to come, yet seemed to think she was the only one who was alright and everyone else was on the verge of a nervous breakdown, going crazy or needing immediate help. In her delusional state she was going to call the pastor, whose church they were leaving, and offer the Watkins' home as a place to live. She thought they would need it, since they may lose their pastorate just as had happened to her and Frank many years before.

Bridget and Priscilla were traumatized many times, yet always it was enforced to them that nobody should be told of the things that were going on at home, especially their mother's mental health. It was supposedly too shameful to share with anyone. In her anguish, Priscilla asked her cousin: "If you were a boy who was interested in dating me, would you not because of my mother's condition?"

He bowed his head and closed his eyes for a moment, then responded. "No, I don't think I would ask to date you." Priscilla remembered that for many years, allowing it to seal her fate of never being good enough to be loved or married.

By the time Margaret's mother, Emily, had heard of the Watkins' decision to no longer attend the main church that had been corporate headquarters prior to the split, she called Margaret with a fierce demand. "Frank is no longer welcome in my home. He has taken you and the girls away from the church, and the Bible teaches 'Wherefore come out from among them, and be ye separate, saith the Lord, and touch not the unclean thing; and I will receive you.' (2 Corinthians 6:17). You and the girls are welcome to come but he cannot come with you."

To this, Margaret wisely replied, "I will not go where he is not welcome. You will have to celebrate Thanksgiving without all of us."

At the same time, the father of one of Priscilla's classmates was of like mind as Frank and Margaret. He was even the president of both the high school and the college at that time but chose to resign his position in order to pursue biblical truth. He met with Frank and some other families with similar views and started a church in the basement of one of the homes in Pleasant Valley. The tiny basement room was quickly remodeled into a little chapel and classroom and about six families started meeting there together. One family had elementary-aged children and the classroom was for them.

The high school and college students had a

much bigger challenge, however. With two students in the group who needed to finish high school and several in varying years of college, Frank and Margaret decided that they would try to put together a last-minute curriculum for high school to help their students graduate and at the same time prepare some classwork to help Bridget get ready for college. Bridget and Priscilla saw it somewhat as a challenging adventure, but Priscilla's heart was broken. The young man she was trying so hard not to love, who reminded her of her father, was deeply entrenched in the original church and school and there was no hope, she knew, for their future. Worse yet, she could not discuss it with anyone, and her mother was quite emotional these days about everything else. For the first time, Priscilla started showing signs of emotional stress herself with severe headaches that would not go away. She felt confused, disillusioned and fearful. She also wondered how this all related to current culture, but certainly could not ask those questions yet.

Chapels and Changes

The Sunday after their life-changing decision, Margaret was unable to resurface to go anywhere to church. Frank realized his responsibility for leading his children spiritually so took them up the mountains to a beautiful little chapel in Green Mountain Falls. The Church in the Wildwood was a welcome solace that morning for the hurting family. For the first time in their lives, they observed the sacrament of Communion. This had never been offered in the Emmanuel Circle of Churches for fear of a person partaking unworthily.

Monday was Labor Day and Frank believed the family needed a trip down to his first pastorate in southeastern Colorado to visit dear family friends from their school days. It was a wonderful diversion from the swirling pain and confusion of home and exactly what the family needed. They traveled there and returned in one day, but on the way home Priscilla started sobbing uncontrollably. Her head throbbed as her life felt like a little red wagon that had been turned upside down with everything inside falling over the edge of a mountain into a ravine. Her loss was more than she could bear.

School started with Priscilla's mother, Margaret, presiding over the home-schooling from American School of Correspondence. Priscilla studied typing, consumer economics, and American history with them. Her Bible training occurred every week at the rented home of the new pastor of a basement church and for English, Priscilla studied in the dark bedroom of an elderly lady's home, adjacent to the school campus where she had attended the previous year. From that window she could watch her friends coming and going to classes and her heart broke into even more tiny pieces. Several weeks later, Priscilla was learning to trust again and enjoyed the freedom and class work that the new schooling situation brought to her. Bridget thrived in the independent study of her college preparatory work and Margaret started to get well again. Frank continued to work and the consistent Biblical teaching every Sunday and Wednesday comforted and encouraged the family.

Spring came and it was time for Priscilla to

graduate from high school. Determined to do their best, her parents and the pastor planned for a simple graduation ceremony in the rented Roswell Community Church on the north end of town. Priscilla wore a white dress, outfitted like her sister the year before. A hand-designed diploma was made by the elderly art teacher who taught English from her home near the old campus. None of her many relatives from the other side of the split, who were living in town, could come to the graduation, as doing so would signal their approval. Her maternal grandmother had fearfully excommunicated the family from any future celebrations back when they had left the church. Things had not changed very much in the past year. To her delight, Priscilla's Aunt Sophie flew in from West Virginia.

The graduation day came and went, and Margaret was careful to have a portrait of Priscilla taken, just as she had done for Bridget. It documented an important milestone in Priscilla's life.

Their new pastor bought land and immediately built a house with an attached chapel that could later be turned back into a garage in the future, if they ever needed for the house to sell. The students also learned that an effort was being made in northern Indiana to prepare a new Bible institute where they could go to college. With anticipation, Priscilla started preparing for this first adventure away from home with Bridget. They planned to go together the following fall, when Priscilla would be a freshman in college and Bridget would be a sophomore. Margaret helped them sew new dresses and shop for dormitory supplies. The girls worked all summer cleaning houses and saved money towards their tuition. A new little guidebook was printed with identical rules to the ones maintained by the Emmanuel Circle of Churches. The day finally came in late September when the caravan bound for Indiana would leave to head east. Priscilla could hardly wait.

Farmhouse Faculty

The northern area of Indiana had nothing in common with the flat prairies of the west. Leaving behind prairies and cattle ranches, as far as the eye could see, against a backdrop of mountains as high as fourteen thousand feet, they were now surrounded by trees, a sluggish river, lush farmland, the scent of hog farms and endless corn.

When they left that late September morning, it was early and not yet light. The pastor and his wife, along with their two sons, spread out among two cars and a moving truck. Bridget, Priscilla and their beloved friend, Anne, traveled with the elderly English teacher—the girls separated from the boys. In this close of quarters, with the blending of four different families, just the trip itself for three days was boot camp in preparation for "dormitory" life.

When they arrived in Indiana, later that week, their excitement was at an all-time high. Not the typical arches of a regular college, but a large, old remodeled farmhouse was their landing place. Out on the northwest side of town in the rural county area was a road with five houses from one intersection to the other. All the rest of the area was covered with either woods or farmland. The two-story farmhouse would be their new academic institution called "Emmanuel Bible Institute". With the front porch turned into a boys' dormitory after it had been winterized and a living room and dining room turned into a library and cafeteria, the upstairs was reserved for the girls. Two boys and four teachers lived downstairs and nine girls and two teachers lived upstairs, with a curtain hung at the top of the stairs for privacy.

The kitchen had a quick redo that made it easier to cook for the little family of seventeen. Adding seven more students in the surrounding county who lived with their families, a tiny school began to form. The teachers were very qualified and taught English, Spanish, Bible, theology, history, literature, Greek, science, sewing and music. A beautiful church that was recently built provided a good assembly area for chapel and weekly church services providing for band and chorus along with a stringed ensemble. The students worked for the lawyers in town, cleaning their homes or offices, and the surrounding countryside was beautiful any season of the year.

It may have been Friday night, but as the two boys left the dormitory to go out for the evening, the remaining students gathered in the study hall to learn the intricate details of how to be good Emmanuel girls. How to dress, how to keep their rooms neat and how to treat the boys. After that, the girls were dismissed for two hours of study and lights out at ten o'clock p.m. This was the usual routine as the weeks slipped from fall into winter and ultimately the beauty of an eastern springtime.

Frogs chorused from the nearby pond and the gentle sounds accompanied by the "twir" of the red-winged blackbird left an indelible memory with the setting sun. Since air conditioning had not yet made its way to this rural dormitory, open windows kept the spring breezes flowing while the girls read their books or typed. Little did Priscilla know that change was in the wind as well.

With the end of the spring semester came a final music program including choral and band music. The girls wore navy dresses with white collars and the boys had their traditional dark pants, white shirts and ties. Special selections of men's quartet or string ensembles added to the evening's beauty. Priscilla and Bridget packed some of their belongings to return west for the summer and happily left for home again.

It was a pivotal summer. Communication was open, honest and painful and their parents trolled the depths of the details the girls shared of their individual perspectives of the past year. While Priscilla seemed to be thriving with the friendships, structure and safety of her Bible-school world, Bridget was languishing in sorrow and despair. The two sisters had uprooted from everything familiar to move to a rural Bible school in an Indiana farmhouse. One evening when they had been on kitchen duty together, Bridget had gone to the basement to retrieve a jar of canned green beans for dinner. There had been a problem in the basement and the boys had been digging it out. Spring rains had raised the water table and murky flood waters lay between the wooden steps and the storage for canned goods on the other side. A wonky timber acted as a bridge across the water and that evening, Priscilla had found Bridget hiding on the timber, sobbing.

The week before, a science school trip had taken

the class to observe a flock of baby chicks and Bridget was devastated by the little outcast bird, who though already struggling to survive, was being pecked by all the others and its feathers were being removed. It was all Bridget could bear. She identified with that little chick and saw herself as different, struggling to survive and attacked by those around her.

Priscilla told her parents about the sad evening. Her parents listened carefully and took their time to guide Bridget into a better life. What would her future hold? Her only options were to be a school teacher or clean houses the rest of her life if she did not get married. The statistics for marriage were not looking good for any of the girls for marriage and an introverted, deep-thinking scientist was more of an exception than the rule. Molds can be so constricting on young people and forcing them into an unnatural path is detrimental. Bridget and her mother spent many hours in conversation and "What if...?"s. Her father steadily worked and provided for the family. Fortunately, one of his medical benefits included insurance for counseling which was a lifesaver for this confusing time.

One healing event during this time was an important visit that Emily, Margaret's mother, made to the home of the Watkins in Pleasant Valley. She had her daughter drive her there, and marching up the sidewalk with her little white purse as if she was taking care of very important business, Emily told Margaret that she was sorry for the way she had treated her about leaving the church and asked Margaret to forgive her. It was a tremendous gift of humility and acceptance that meant the world to the whole family.

Margaret decided that the time had come to take a risk for the sake of the girls. She enrolled at the local university and took an English class to feel out what it might be like as an option for Bridget. She was pleased. She enjoyed the mental stimulation, the respect she received in spite of her conservative dress and the takeaways of writing that were insightful and cathartic for her personally.

As July ended, it was time for a drastic decision. Priscilla stood in the kitchen doorway watching her mother doing the laundry. Margaret was crying as she said emphatically, "We're through! We are never going back to that church again!" Priscilla was horrified, shocked and terrified, all in equal parts.

"Where does that leave me?" she queried.

"You can do whatever you want", her mother

replied. "You are eighteen and we cannot keep you here. If you want to return to school you can, but Bridget will not be going with you. After being enrolled at the university she will be studying chemistry. It is the best thing for her mental health and personal freedom. We have not been accepted at church for this decision. In fact, the rejection Bridget is experiencing behooves us to leave with her so she will not be cast out without loving support." Truth be told, this would not be that devastating for either Frank or Margaret since their entrance to the Emmanuel Circle of Churches had not occurred until their early and mid-teen years. They knew life existed outside the confines of the controlling church. They had experienced faith, family happiness and options and had not forgotten how those things were.

Priscilla, however, was shafted.

Providentially Hindered

Priscilla's parents remained loyal. They studied both girls carefully and attempted to meet their unique needs in appropriate ways. Often Frank would invite Priscilla to go for a ride up on the ridge overlooking Pleasant Valley. There they would watch the sunset and talk about the conflict going on at home. Priscilla would tearfully express her anger and fear at the changes coming between her and Bridget. Most of all she would lament over her relationship with her mother and how sure she was that her mother did not understand her circumstances or feelings. Carefully and prayerfully Frank would listen, advise and correct.

Margaret could be found at home on her knees by Priscilla's bed, recommitting her to God repeatedly. Bridget blossomed. She found creative ways to gently modify her wardrobe without cutting her hair or wearing pants. Cute plaid skirts, sweaters, socks and penny loafers made her look particularly charming as she curled up by the kitchen table to study her organic chemistry. Her countenance became more and more serene and at peace. Her confidence gave her more love to share with those around her.

Baffled by the changes, Priscilla doggedly kept her focus on the return to the farmhouse at the end of the summer. There she would find safety in the cloister, away from the din of options. Driven by this fear, Priscilla continued to prepare. She and her father decided that they would drive back together in his little pick-up and go by way of his family in West Virginia to pay a visit to his grandmother.

The silver ribbon of interstate that lay across the state of Kansas brought with it some singular physical challenges. Sickness along the way required frequent stops at out-of-the-way service stations and dingy bathrooms with keys to the external entrances off the parking lot, but Priscilla pressed on, determined that her sickness would subside once the swirl of change was behind her and she would be separated by twelve hundred miles. It didn't.

After a sweet (and final) visit to her great-grandmother in West Virginia, her father u-turned back to Indiana and said goodbye to his baby daughter. Relieved and terrified, she watched him drive away.

Up in the garret Priscilla adjusted to her two new roommates. One was suffering much as she was, with pain in her back that left her collapsed on her bed often in tears, though she was one of the most dedicated, conscientious workers on the team. When Priscilla looked back on their plight later, she wondered if all that pain was related to the internal mental anguish the girls had experienced.

The abdominal pain and gastric distress continued as Priscilla started her classes and picked up her schedule of early morning devotions, daily chapel, classes, working, homework, music and regular church services. She enjoyed being with her friends again and always found a rousing game of volleyball in the field by the church to be exciting. It was not long, though, until she began missing classes and one "sick day", while in bed in her room, the dean of women came to tell her the president and his wife were on their way to visit her in her room. Soon they arrived and with great kindness assured her of their concern and love for her. They had been dear friends with her parents in Bible school when both the president and her father were preparing for the ministry.

"If you were our daughter, we would want you to come home," they advised. This was even more poignant to Priscilla because she knew they had a daughter her age. "We have made arrangements with your parents and will be taking you to the airport in Indianapolis on Wednesday for you to fly home. If your health returns, you can come back to school next semester." After they left her room, Priscilla burst into tears. She felt she had failed. The struggle to be strong seemed to have gotten the best of her. It had been such a marathon of perseverance through the past weeks as church leaders had advised her that she should leave home and never return to such bad influences.

The Bible admonishes that we should "[t]rain up a child in the way he should go: and when he is old, he will not depart from it" (Proverbs 22:6). Whether it is the way he should really go or not, it is very hard to depart from it!

When Priscilla returned to her home that fateful day, an odd twist had occurred. Her sister had chicken pox and since neither girl had been vaccinated it was decided that Priscilla should stay with her grandmother and aunts until Bridget improved. This ended up helping ease Priscilla back into the overwhelming situation in a bit of a neutral way as her body healed. Tensions mounted as Sundays came and went. Margaret, Frank and Bridget attended a lovely Wesleyan chapel outside the city limits while Priscilla swung between the churches involved in the first and second splits. She hated attending the church that met in the garage of a home built specifically as a temporary meeting place, yet she loved the people there. She felt alone, ashamed and afraid of the future.

Little did she know what God had in store for her that would be prove his providential plan for her future.

Protection from Family

Priscilla languished in confusion, anger and fear those first months back home. Not only was she miserable about where to go to church, she felt abandoned and jealous that Bridget's needs were more urgent than her own. She felt inferior intellectually to her sister and wondered if she was as gifted, would she be able to follow the same path? Her high school years and graduation had been cut short by the first church split and that unfinished business of an unaccredited high school diploma shamed and embarrassed her. Though her mother offered repeatedly for her to take a GED and enroll at the local community college or university, she was too afraid that she would only prove to herself that she could not succeed in the real world of academia.

She received phone calls from her former teachers and friends in the community where she had attended Bible school the two years previously. Sometimes they would disguise their voice on the telephone to get past her parents and talk to her, telling her how dangerous it was to remain at home. They told her that her family was lost, hell-bound and would bring her with them. Other times they wrote letters, telling her the same. The worst day of all was when her entire wardrobe was shipped home for her to continue dressing as was directed by the Emmanuel Circle of Churches. Though she was thankful for the time and love that went into its return by the Bible school's leadership, she was saddened by the bondage it represented. She also felt deceitful, because she was beginning to wonder how long she could continue representing that lifestyle. At three different points that fall, winter and spring she stayed with different aunts to escape the conflict at home. Their homes, like her own because they were her mother's sisters, provided neutral environments of love and security. Still, the ever-present under-current of "which church is right" was stressful because the stakes were so high for adapting to a different theology and lifestyle.

The next summer Frank was shopping for a new suit at the mall. He was looking for a dark one, of course, with a dark tie and a white shirt. In a small menswear shop in the local mall, the proprietor asked him, "Are you a minister?"

"No, but I used to be."

"Interesting. My wife works at a children's ministry here in town that partners with many churches around the world."

"How unusual," Frank replied. "My daughter just mentioned to us at home recently about seeing this sign out on Austin Bluffs Parkway with a tagline, 'Caring for needy children around the world in the name of Jesus'. It seems the name of the organization was 'Compassion'."

"That's it!" Mr. Howard replied. "Here is my wife's name. She is the administrative assistant to the president. Maybe she could give your daughter a tour." Through this ordinary interchange, God was orchestrating a tectonic plate shift in Priscilla's life. Her life would never be the same again.

It was only a matter of days until Priscilla was standing at the front desk waiting for Lena Howard to come down from the president's office to meet her in the lobby. She was going to take her on a tour of the office and explain about the ministry of Compassion International, Inc., through the pictures, video and history on exhibit in the lovely building. It had been there for five years after moving from Chicago in 1980. Beautiful pictures of children smiling, drinking pure water or caring for their family's goat graced the walls as artwork. Lena explained the history of Compassion starting in South Korea during the war and helping to care for the many orphans left from those difficult days. She talked about how the organization had grown and what its mission and purpose had become. At the end, she offered Priscilla a golden ticket. She asked her if she would be interested in volunteering at the ministry to learn more about it. Priscilla was thrilled and decided to start coming regularly to help with mailings, filing or sorting.

One day she was surprised in the human resources office by the question, "Would you like to take a typing test? In order to work here, you need to be able to type and do accurate data entry. Why don't you practice on this computer every day after you volunteer and then you can check on your progress?"

Priscilla gave it her best and practiced. When it was time to take her test, she passed and was offered a job as a clerk in the estate planning department. She learned how to assist the managers who were caring for sponsors' bequests to Compassion in the form of wills, trusts, annuities and other large gifts. She could not believe the opportunity that opened right in her own backyard.

Friends from the interior of the Emmanuel Circle of Churches continued to contact her. Former teachers, the pastor's wife, even a very kind suitor who brought a long-stemmed rose and card to her office one day. She was torn. So much safety and good lay behind her, but so much more possibility lay ahead. Strictly conditioned to please people, especially those in leadership, Priscilla writhed with the choices that only she could make. She wasn't even sure she knew what she wanted, let alone how to express it. Her fear made her want to play both sides to avoid offending anyone, but that only made everyone more confused and miserable.

A true light dawned in her dimmed spirit one Wednesday after attending the weekly chapel at Compassion's corporate office. A speaker from East Asia was talking about a group of blind children who were hearing the gospel for the first time and were particularly listening to the Bible verse, "The people that walked in darkness have seen a great light: they that dwell in the land of the shadow of death, upon them hath the light shined" (Isaiah 9:2). He continued to explain the joy that came to the blind children as they perceived the truth of God's love for them, demonstrated through His Son's death on the cross and how that essence of the gospel shed light on their physically darkened lives. She was spellbound.

That evening, she returned as usual to the regular prayer meeting that met in the garage of her Emmanuel pastor's home and she was a bit hurried as she left to go. She realized that her dress might have shrunk a bit from washing, but she did not bother to change to a longer one, tired of playing that game. She also realized that she was giving in to the convenience of normal pantyhose that did not have seams down the back as expressly required in the church guidebook.

The next day she received a call from the pastor's wife, warning her of the dangers of her new job and of the worldly appearance that she had when she came to prayer meeting that night. Suddenly it did not seem so important anymore. The world seemed so much bigger than the twenty or so people gathered in the garage church. The issues at stake seemed much bigger, too. In that moment, she realized that she did not want to ever go back to church there again. She was not sure where she would go or what she would do, but she knew there was going to be a change.

Even though she had been advised by the pastor's wife to not talk or eat lunch with her new friends who worked at Compassion, Priscilla still responded to their gentle overtures of friendship and broke down a few times to share her sack lunch with them. One lady, in charge of all the time-cards and payroll, invited Priscilla to go to church with her. Priscilla went home and told Bridget about the invitation and the girls realized they had both met people they respected, both at the university and at Compassion, from the same church, so they decided it was worth a try.

If the Bible was what they needed, the Bible was what they got. In the non-flashy chapel that they visited they found rich Bible teaching, music, dedicated families, hearts for missions and a total lack of political drama. The elders who cared for the spiritual flock took their work seriously and made a point to ask Priscilla and Bridget if they had ever placed their faith in Jesus Christ and if they were certain about how they would enter heaven one day. Lots of meals in their homes, games and movies and picnics later, both girls were baptized in this wonderful church that was showing them the blessed truth of scripture alone with all the trappings peeled back.

In Compassion's office, the soft, burlap cubbies provided a quiet learning zone for the new employee. There was so much to absorb. She could discreetly overhear not only the mores for how to answer the telephone correctly, but also the softer skills of how to spend the lunch hour on payday. It seemed exhausting...all the listening, processing and filtering consumed her time and energy. References to current culture such as past or current television shows, songs that were topping the charts or favorite movies of the weekend left her blindsided. She tried to cover her ignorance, but it always seemed to show through. She tried to joke about it, but that soon seemed lame and quickly lost its impact. It was humiliating to keep explaining her past and her present. Some found it novel, some were intrigued, and others were just plain nosy. Still, Priscilla patiently answered all their questions and tried to give reasons for why she lived the way she did and why she was ignorant of so much in her current culture. Each day she braided her hair, neatly pinned it around her head like the intricate border of an apple pie. She continued to try to find outfits that were less homemade looking and made the most of her skirts and blouses. She reconsidered the necessity of black vs. nude pantyhose and made the bold decision that maybe that was not a critical infraction of the moral code anymore. Floundering through her countless questions of true right and wrong she became more and more thankful for the friends who were forming around her–genuine, mature Christians who valued her for who she was and looked past her exterior.

Across the hall from her office, she kept noticing a lovely, tall young lady who seemed just a bit older than her. Regal, tender and very professional, Priscilla admired her tremendously. One day the two of them met in the restroom in front of the mirror when she asked, "Where have you grown up going to church? You look very much like I did at your age."

Suddenly, Priscilla felt very known. She got to know the young lady's name, Claire, and the two decided they would spend more time together in the future. They had great fun zooming around town in Claire's adorable red hatchback. They went hiking, had Saturday morning breakfast out, went shopping, cooked together and talked about life in general. Priscilla could not get over the gift she was being given in this wonderful friend who understood and loved her unconditionally. She found that the more her heart was warmed by that love, the easier it was to trust God more fully. The more she trusted God, the more she trusted His children whom she worked with every day. It became easier to have lunch in the lunchroom with them or run to Dairy Queen on a break.

The Long and The Short of It ~ Hair

One day Priscilla made a bold fashion move. She went to work with her hair freshly washed and unbraided, cascading around her shoulders and below her waist. She was not prepared for the attention it brought, especially from the men in the office. She received compliments all day and was so upset by her actions that she could not wait to get it back up in its familiar pie the next day. One message she did hear during that experiment was that a woman's hair is a glory to her and that seemed to carry no guilt.

The next two years provided happiness and growth for the family, albeit there was still a valiant struggle. Honesty became easier and courage was worked out like a healthy muscle. Independence, a very unfamiliar attitude, began to feel safer. There seemed to be more breathing room at the family dinner table as topics ranged from theology to chemistry to social justice. Judgement and condemnation were less of a reflex in conversation and as Margaret and Frank became more secure in their new-found worship experiences, grounded in Biblical theology, an unexpected side effect was happening at the same time. Margaret was getting well. The mental torture of years of constricting lifestyle and manipulative church environment was replaced by grace, scripture, worship, new friendship and the freedom to love others.

Frank began a six-year journey of comparing his Armenian theological background to his newly found Calvinistic environment and searched scripture to develop his own beliefs on the subject, even though he had spent many years of Bible school training, ministry and pastoring in an Armenian church. Bridget and Priscilla enjoyed spending time together because their worlds had become so large there was plenty of room for them in the same universe and their competition started to melt away.

Bridget's attractive character and intellect soon captured the attention of a dashing young man from the south who was graduating from the Air Force Academy. His winsome courtship of her eventually led to an engagement that prompted a significant cultural crisis. The ring! For three generations on both sides now, no jewelry had been worn, even a wedding ring. The "wearing of gold" was forbidden, "Whose adorning let it not be that outward adorning of plaiting the hair, and of wearing of gold, or of putting on of apparel..." (1 Peter 3:3), but Bridget was prepared. She knew what was coming and talked it over with her parents. Consequently, when she showed up in the vestibule of their church one Sunday evening after a delightful romp in the aspen when she had said "yes", her parents gave their full approval, though not without some unsettling shock. A few months later, Margaret herself asked Frank to place a wedding ring on her finger. He did so one Sunday morning by the piano in the living room on the way to church. She wanted there to be no question that she was his married wife.

Priscilla realized that she would soon be the maid of honor for her sister's wedding, which brought her to important crossroads Would she want to be eternally remembered as wearing her hair in that familiar pie at the wedding?

In addition, her health was challenging her again, this time with fierce headaches and boils on her scalp from the long hair. Ovarian cysts and abdominal pain made it impossible to stand up sometimes. In the process, her doctor recommended a hysterectomy and scheduled it a few weeks out, giving her time to arrange coverage at work. The day before the surgery, something unexpected happened. The vice president of Compassion asked her to come to his open office. He wanted to pray with her before her surgery; after all, he was the director of the division in which she worked. He prayed for healing and committed her future to God's hands. Priscilla was dumbfounded. She was not used to anyone ever praying for healing in faith that it might happen. The God she served was much too severe for that kind of mercy. Off she went to the pre-op appointment with her mother and to everyone's surprise, the ultrasound showed such a notable shrinkage of the cysts that the doctor decided to cancel the surgery, accepting the risk that any malignancy could have ruptured and spread. But God had chosen to heal Priscilla because this sickness was not as serious as she had thought. "This sickness is not unto death, but for the glory of God, that the Son of God might be glorified thereby" (John 19:30) appeared on the computer monitor's Bible-verse-of-the-day when she surprised her friends by reappearing for work. A few weeks later the staff watched a film on the sanctity of a baby's life and

Priscilla wept at the thought of still having hope for motherhood someday.

Spring came and with it the exciting preparations for Bridget's wedding. There were bridesmaid dresses to complete, flowers to prepare and music and invitations to coordinate. Priscilla continued to spend time with her friend Claire, learning how to dress and relate to this newfound culture that had surrounded her all along but not been imbibed. She joined the church choir with Bridget, and they delighted in the work involved in preparing for an Easter cantata. The words were deeply meaningful to her as she contemplated them further, away from the trappings of all her good deeds and righteous appearance

"But we are all as an unclean thing, and all our righteousnesses are as filthy rags; and we all do fade as a leaf; and our iniquities, like the wind, have taken us away" (Isaiah 64:6).

On Good Friday, Priscilla had the day off and she went to the salon with Claire, who was getting her hair cut in preparation for Easter weekend. While there, Priscilla also asked for her hair to be cut, not knowing the meaning of any of the important terms: trimmed, feathered, bangs, inches. She had been thinking about it for many months.

Priscilla had read many books about young women who devoted their lives to helping children. It had become her lifelong goal to do the same. She was inspired by Jane Addams, who started the Hull-House in Chicago. The life of Amy Carmichael who went to India to mother children involved in temple prostitution also increased her desire to serve her present generation. As Priscilla's desire grew to work with inner city children, the less she could tolerate the idea of how her appearance could be perceived as bigoted, standoffish or even unattractive to the children she would want to reach for Jesus. When she imagined herself walking the streets of downtown Chicago, Los Angeles or Denver, clothed in long skirts, long sleeves and long hair, she dreaded all the explanations required to begin a conversation with a mother or her children. She felt she would be a stumbling block and a distraction. To that end, she felt motivated to make such a significant change.

As she looked at the floor and saw sixteen inches of thick brown hair lying around her, she started to cry. What had she just done? This was an irreversible risk and there was not going to be any gluing it back in place. Walking through the back door to meet her mother at home was the worst moment of the whole weekend. Though her mother was shocked, and a bit upset, Priscilla was not condemned. Her mother just told her it would grow back, and she would not have to make the same mistake again.

That Sunday was the most glorious and memorable Easter of Priscilla's life. Standing in the choir as she sang the powerful truths of the death and resurrection of Jesus had brilliant meaning to her. She stood naked before her Creator, haircut and all. She pondered the fact that His last words were, "It is finished" and she knew there was nothing more she needed to add to be worthy of His great salvation.

"When Jesus therefore had received the vinegar, he said, It is finished: and he bowed his head, and gave up the ghost" (John 19:30).

She was His child and that would never be any more or any less true than it was in this moment. The joy and peace were complete and unforgettable.

As the crab apple blossoms faded and the lilacs bloomed, Margaret was supportive and organized in preparation for the upcoming wedding. Bridget and her fiancé were still in college studying hard and Bridget was just not that interested in obsessing over such trivia. In her laid-back fashion, she kept her eyes on her man and her schoolwork and prepared for her marriage instead of her wedding. She chose an exquisite Jessica McClintock gown that complimented her long brown hair, softly styled in a knot at the back of her head. Her simplicity and purity shown from her countenance as she and her new husband walked under the arch of drawn swords held by his friends from the Air Force Academy. She beamed with her spray of deep, red roses and as they left for their honeymoon after the wedding, Priscilla felt bereft of her very dear friend and sister. She felt replaced and displaced and though she wished she could have hidden it, the emotional impact manifested itself physically, as usual.

While adjusting to their immediate move to the southeast for his military assignment, Priscilla threw herself into her work and decided it might be worth dipping her toe into the waters of academia again. Too stubborn to take a GED and be proven ignorant, she found a way to sign up for a class at the state university and simply be an undeclared major.

Somehow, they let her in for a sociology class one semester and a psychology class the second. To her shock, she enjoyed the classes and found that she could survive and finish them without self-destructing while she worked full-time. This was a major confidence boost and she had hope for a possible college degree in the distant future.

This also seemed like a good time to take another independent step – moving out into her own apartment. She selected one right next to Claire, because she told it her it was available. Though simply furnished, she enjoyed this new freedom and an opportunity to work on her personal emotional growth alone and gain perspective in healing family relationships.

Part V

Broken and Spilled Out

Of Closed Doors and Open Windows

Priscilla had not yet embraced the fact that her path could be different than Bridget's. At the Presbyterian Church which she attended with her parents, after Bridget's marriage and moving away, Priscilla started singing in the choir with them and enjoying it very much.

While she was there, she started to notice a young Air Force Academy graduate, William, who was now an officer, and seemed to also share her love for choir and all music. They attended the singles ministry together, and one Sunday after church he asked her if she would like to go out for lunch with him. This sounded interesting and harmless, so she decided to accept. During that time, they would go to cultural events, make homemade sausage together, watch "Star Wars" or cook gourmet dinners.

One memorable evening William invited her over to his apartment for a special dinner he cooked himself. Delicious broiled salmon was arranged on the dinner plate beside a bundle of steamed asparagus spears which had been tied with a thin strip of lemon zest. A cheery bouquet of daffodils formed the centerpiece with two tickets to the evening's entertainment tucked under the vase of the flowers. They would be going to see a live play, "Frankenstein", later that evening. He was extremely sensitive and moved by the aesthetics around him and this also was attractive to Priscilla.

Sharing his Nikon camera kit with her, William inspired Priscilla to take a trip by herself to Europe. He had been there and mastered the German language, and his love for the Alps and the beauty of the countryside made her want to take the risk.

Priscilla tried to get her Aunt Sophie to go with her, to which her single aunt replied: "Oh, you are just going to go off and get married and will never travel abroad like I have done!" In response, whether she said it or not, Priscilla's attitude was, "Try me!" That summer began with a memorable week of traveling the farmlands of Switzerland, Austria and Germany with a group of senior citizens, all who adopted her as their own.

A quizzical observation Priscilla had made was that William never talked about their future together. After all, the main goal in relationships between men and women in her church background was for there to be limited physical contact. His reservation and slowness in that area appeared seemingly safe to her and she continued to spend time with him for over a year. So, one summer afternoon, when they were hiking in the foothills, she asked William what he thought their future would look like.

William planned a dinner later in the week to vaguely talk about it at a charming Alpine restaurant. Still, never having asked for a kiss or held her hand more than one time, she was puzzled by his behavior. He came to her home the next Sunday evening while her parents were at church and sat down beside her, laying his arm over the back of the couch around her shoulder.

"I have something really difficult to share about our future," he began. "The reason this has been moving so slowly is because I really have homosexual tendencies and do not ever see how I can be married. My Christian counselor suggested I appear to be dating and I have actually had three of you waiting in the wings all at the same time."

Priscilla reeled in shock internally. She had

grown to care about him very much over the past year. He was certainly freer than her in many ways but his tender heart and compassion towards her had been significant encouragement. He had not scared her with aggressive sensuality and that seemed safe to her though somewhat confusing. She knew he truly had faith, because he had helped her own faith grow. His heart was heavy because he felt sad and helpless to overcome it and her heart went out to him. Never again would she look at homosexuality the same way the rest of her life. It now had a face, a name and a person she deeply respected.

With this occurring before it was acceptable to disclose sexual orientation within the military, she was strictly forbidden to tell anyone. For several days she had no idea what to do, but ultimately wrote him a letter that expressed how she was unable to continue in the relationship. He responded with a letter including multiple scriptures admonishing her to not be fearful, but she was unprepared to take the risk of a continued pseudo-relationship. His dream of opening a gourmet restaurant on the northeast coast in a lighthouse after exiting the military and graduating from culinary school appealed to her. In fact, she had bargained with God often in prior months about how surely, she could figure out a way to do inner city ministry to children on a shore in Massachusetts somewhere. However, the unmistakable conviction in her soul to not veer from the path of her calling to urban ministry kept her focused. After the pain started to subside, she knelt by her bed one evening and knew clearly as she prayed that nothing could come between her and her heavenly Father's leading for her future. She had already done her absolute best to copy her big sister and please her parents, and in so doing it had all completely unraveled. Now she was ready to obey God's plan for her whatever the cost.

The "El" Stands for L O V E

While Priscilla continued to enjoy her employment with Compassion International, Inc., new opportunities came her way. A secretarial position for the director of sponsor relations came up and she applied for the job. After working in estate planning and moving to customer service in both letter writing and answering telephones, she was ready to take on a greater challenge with more influence providing the best sponsor experience possible for the organization's valuable donors. A new director had recently been hired from Atlanta and she became his secretary. The new position brought additional friendships and more professional freedom.

It was during this time that a lively, young executive from Chicago came to visit Compassion's chapel and tell about the partnering ministry that was beginning in the United States in urban areas. The work of Compassion had only been in developing countries and more recently the Native

American areas were being included. Priscilla was incredibly inspired by the presentation and talked to him afterwards. He casually mentioned that their ministry, Inner City Impact, based in Chicago, was looking for an Executive Secretary to the founder and president. She researched the ministry some more, talked with the staff who were directly connected in the partnership and decided to apply. Later that summer she was invited to a job interview in the Denver airport. Since the president's wife worked for United Airlines, he could easily fly wherever he needed, saving travel dollars for the ministry. The airport was a logical place for the interview. Meeting him and interviewing was positive and enjoyable, and Priscilla returned home to wait. And wait some more. She had already pursued opportunities in Denver, Kansas City and Los Angeles, but this one motivated her in a way the others did not.

Soon Priscilla was invited for another interview in Chicago, onsite in their offices, and they flew her there for the visit in late July, of 1989. This was a monumental trip for Priscilla. It was a culmination of all of her dreams coming true in a matter of a few days. It was also a heart-rending time of reality settling into the very platelets of her blood. The staff at Inner City Impact were busy, independent and all used to pushing themselves beyond their comfort zone. It was just what they did. It was a good thing, because they would not be fussing over Priscilla if she moved there, so they initiated her with an interesting test.

She was to fly into O'Hare airport and take the elevated train (The El) from there to the California stop a few miles northwest of downtown. There she was supposed to come down from the train platform, out the station and wait on the sidewalk for a staff member, whom she had never met, to pick her up. She had never been in the city before, and she felt afraid they would not recognize her in the crowd. She need never have feared. The naive girl that stepped off the curb and into the waiting car was wearing a mint green shirt and skirt with white shoes. Her conservative appearance screamed "outsider" and she punctuated it by exclaiming as she settled in the car, "It's the ghetto! It is just like the ghetto I have always dreamed of working in someday!" Soon she would learn how inappropriate those initial comments really were.

A patient veteran, Terry, who was picking her

up, took her to a charming older Swedish home that had an apartment upstairs. It was in Humboldt Park and had a country charm in its decor that immediately made Priscilla feel welcome. Moreover, Terry was full of character, kindness and experience and Priscilla admired her. Soon she was meeting the staff at the corporate office, visiting the neighborhoods to the northwest and south of Chicago where other areas had field offices for Inner City Impact. Best of all, she visited the clubs that met after school where the children came to play games, learn scripture and character-building principles, experience leadership training or prepare for camp. She was amazed by all the staff; their commitment, unselfishness and unconditional love made her want to be a part of their team.

One event of the interview weekend was a planned staff celebration for a birthday at the home of one of the full-time missionaries, straight west in the city near Oak Park. It was the day before a week-long camping trip was planned in Michigan and the missionaries and summer staff would be taking one hundred children to camp in two school busses. The night before, however, they took time out to fellowship together over a birthday cake for one of the missionaries and Priscilla was invited by Terry to be present there as well.

Priscilla consciously dug her left hand deep into her skirt pocket, determined that none of these young people would know whether she was married, engaged or single. She was determined to never be hurt as badly again as she had been several years before.

What she was completely unprepared for was a tall, young man there from Oregon who had eyes the color of the Pacific Ocean and unruly, light-brown curls. He was friendly, sincere and whenever she purposefully moved to a different part of the house to be sure she was not showing her interest, she would find him there also. They talked about their families, their faith and their shared struggle of growing up with a mother who suffered with illness. She included him in her goodbyes to the group who were going to camp the next day and headed back to the apartment in Humboldt Park with Terry.

The following day Priscilla prepared to return home but was offered the job before she left. She eagerly accepted and flew back to the west to begin packing and moving to Chicago the following month. When she was telling her mother about her trip, the one heartfelt description she gave her was of the young man from Oregon. "He's husband quality, Mamma, really he is. And I will never see him again."

Priscilla's final month at Compassion was full of encouragement and difficult goodbyes. It seemed that everyone in the city who had ever loved her decided that this was the time to tell her so. Even young men suspiciously came out of the woodwork as if they might be interested in getting to know her better since it was relatively safe to say so now that she was moving across the country. Most memorable of all, was when she was called to the president's office because he had received a letter from sponsors indicating how thankful they were for the way Priscilla had thoroughly answered their questions on the phone one day when they had called for clarification about their sponsored child. Even though she was getting ready to leave the office to start her vacation, she had stayed late to help the sponsor and it had not gone unnoticed.

"What I don't understand," began Mr. Everett, "is that I spent so many years trying to get Compassion out of Chicago and you are going right back there!" He went on to say how happy he was for her to be joining Compassion's ministry in this new way and just reminded her to be very careful. Melaku was another leader who took her out for lunch to encourage her on her way. He was a pastor who had moved to the United States from Ethiopia and had a huge soul for advocacy as he served leadership around the world in multiple developing countries. Priscilla was humbled by the outpouring of support and it carried her for many months and years in the difficult times ahead.

Her friends in the singles group in Sunday school were warm and supportive, making every effort to get her address and phone number and be sure to stay in touch. Her mentors encouraged her to look for a good church and singles group in the big city to avoid getting lost in the transition.

Priscilla did not find much resistance from her mother. Their relationship had been challenging at times through the years and perhaps there was a subtle hope in both that the distance would give needed space and mutual respect. Most importantly, however, Priscilla knew that her love for children and missions came directly from her mother who had talked about it all of Priscilla's years of growing up and nurtured her interest in following that path.

Her father, Frank, spoke loudly through his silence of how he really felt about the upcoming change. Understanding her desire and fully aware of the consequences, he had a meaningful conversation with Priscilla about it one evening. She got right to the point.

"You know that I consider you to be my protector and provider until I am married. How do you really feel about me moving to Chicago?" Priscilla asked. "Because I respect your authority placed over me by God, I will not go if you do not want me to."

This put Frank in a difficult position. He was not sure how to answer and as usual, took his time in order to not speak unwisely in haste. "I would never tell you that you cannot go, Priscilla, because I would not want to hinder you from following God's will for your life. However, I will not take you there. You have to get there on your own."

After that was out in the open, Priscilla knew what she had to do. She began organizing her small stash of belongings into things to keep and things to store. She already knew she had a single bed available in the apartment she would be renting with Terry. She packed lightly, with just the things she would need in a fully furnished flat and filled the hatchback of her Toyota Starlet with her belongings. A devoted friend from the singles ministry at her church offered to drive to Chicago with her and fly back on her own.

Anticipation and deep peace held Priscilla steady as she embarked on her new adventure. Up until that summer, she had never met a single person who lived in Chicago and even when she moved, she barely knew her new boss and roommate.

Meanwhile, in that busy month of packing and organizing, a small detail brought a curious result. Priscilla forwarded her mail to her new address. One evening she received a phone call from Terry. "You must have forwarded your mail to your new address. Do you remember that young man, Daniel, from Oregon? He asked me for your address, but the letter he sent to you has showed up here."

Priscilla tried hard to cover her delight. The last thing she wanted was for the new staff in her office to think the only reason she was moving to Chicago was for a prospect of marriage. As soon as she hung up the telephone with Terry, after maintaining her most professional phone etiquette, she headed straight to her mother with the news. "Mamma! I told you he was husband quality, and I thought I would never hear from him again! Maybe he found me as interesting as I found him."

Once moved, Priscilla jumped right into her new role with boundless enthusiasm, a protective layer of naivete and a deep love for the people around her. She was excited by the scintillating sounds of the city and the constant motion and dynamics swirling about her. She had a treacherous learning curve, and if there had been any going back, she would have found a way. For example, the simple act of looking up a telephone number required searching through eight telephone directories, and that required knowing the basic geography of Chicagoland in order to open the correct directory. The brilliant mind of the executive director briefly slept, so the work that he generated through his multitudes of ideas was more than enough to fill an eight-hour day. He could be up at four o'clock a.m., dictating another chapter in the book he was writing before preparing for the next board meeting and planning a fundraising event for generous donors, all before arriving in the office from the suburbs before eight o'clock in the morning. He had impeccable standards and took his leadership very seriously yet with a sensitive and tender heart.

The missionaries who made up the staff of Inner City Impact came from many different backgrounds. Some were single, others married, most were young, all lived in the city limits and the very neighborhood in which they were assigned. It helped them focus on the local church and school and it also saved travel time and conflict of interest. They washed their laundry at the same laundromat where their children's families could be seen and shopped at the same stores. The transit system was not to be feared but to be trusted and used to avoid costly parking tickets and hassles on narrow streets. Festivals drew the missionaries into the surrounding culture and after a week of Puerto Rican days in the early summer, one could never forget the satisfying flavor of Café Bustelo or rice and beans. The emblems on the flag were etched in memory as well as the catchy dance music that belted from the cars that carried the flags.

The heat in the summer was oppressive and air conditioners were far and few between. Priscilla became immersed in her neighborhood with the windows open and the sights, sounds and smells wafted through the spinning fans. Sometimes she would just watch for hours as she observed gang members leaping over fences, running from the police or being corralled at a street corner and loaded into a paddy wagon. Other times she would duck below the window sill when she heard shots fired below. One evening she returned home from work and parked her car curbside to walk towards her little two-flat. Suddenly she was surrounded by five menacing gang members taunting, "You can't park here. This is our street!"

"Yes, I can" she responded without fear. "That is where I live, right there in that apartment, and I am coming home from work." She got out of her car, walked towards the sidewalk and they melted into the early evening shadows.

The assault on Priscilla's senses was never-ending. Sometimes it was the smell of urine and orange peels in the subway station or the sound of cockfights illegally being conducted in the backyards. Other times her eyes longed to be spared from the shocking graffiti with unmistakable body parts and disrespectful profanity blatantly plastered along the railroad bridges. One night she awoke swearing and was shocked that the constant suppression of her environment every day was making its way into her dreams at night and verbally through her lips. What faith it took to believe that God was still holding tightly to her during all the change! She knew she could not afford to go home for Christmas, and it was a good thing, because as the honeymoon period of her adventure wore off, it would have been easy to give up and not come back out of fear.

Instead, her aunt and grandparents in West Virginia sent her money to take Amtrak there to celebrate. Boarding the train in Grand Central Station in Chicago was easy enough and riding along through the frigid night stopping in town after town seemed like a scene from an old movie. Bitter cold iced the windows, making it very difficult to track progress along the route. Somewhere in Ohio the entire train came to a grinding halt and Greyhound busses arrived to disperse the remaining passengers. Hours behind schedule, they arrived in Charleston, West Virginia, and she had the special privilege of seeing the first home her grandparents and aunt had been able to purchase the year before.

Priscilla was tremendously excited when her Aunt Sophie came to the train station to get her off the bus. What a relief it was! She was eager to see her grandparents up in the mountains. Once there, they made plans for a candlelight worship service on Christmas Eve. At that time there was still no television in her grandparents' home. She had a VHS about her work in the urban ministry and wanted to share it with them.

The Christmas Eve service was a precious time of faith and family comfort for Priscilla as she knelt at the altar with Aunt Sophie and they sang "Silent Night" while holding their little candles. However, after borrowing and heaving a large portable TV/VCR unit home from the church, her grandpa would not allow the evil piece of equipment in the house. They meekly took it back to the car and abandoned the idea.

After the infilling of love and kindness that Christmas, Aunt Sophie and Priscilla's grandmother spent the better part of a day packing up supplies to send back to Chicago on the train. They gathered warm hats, mittens, socks and Christian children's literature from the bookstore where Aunt Sophie worked. Priscilla was happy to return and felt renewed purpose and accountability after spending time with family. The snow buried Chicago's drab streets with a temporary blanket of purity and quickly melted into chunky ice as the winds blew in from Lake Michigan. Sometimes as Priscilla walked to work in the mornings, the wind and air were so cold it hurt down in her lungs. She was thankful for the good friends at the mission who surrounded her, always looking for ways to make her feel welcome.

Priscilla continued to prepare for board meetings, transcribe dictation, help the executive director edit his books, send out memos and greeting cards to the staff, coordinate travel for the missionary recruiting trips and stay in touch with the donors who contributed significant amounts of money or gifts in kind to the mission. Any chance she had out of the office to be on the street with the children, there she was. She enjoyed the weekly, third – fifth grade, after-school program for the girls who met at the mission in Humboldt Park. She admired the full-time staff who raised support to work with the girls. She loved the way they could lead songs, games and Bible studies that were engaging and motivated the students to return. It humbled her to watch the prayer walks that were conducted throughout the neighborhood, when the staff quietly walked the streets praying for the safety of the children; that the vices of gang violence and alcohol and drugs would stop stealing the lives of the people who lived there. These times gave her a deep sense of contentment that she was exactly where she was supposed to be and living the dream of her lifetime.

Priscilla received occasional letters from her new acquaintance in Oregon. She noticed a singular trademark on every envelope. Neatly edging the back dip of the envelope after it was sealed, a scripture verse was neatly printed by hand. He encouraged her with each letter. Best of all, the contents inside the letters was showing her the type of man behind the tidy handwriting and pertinent scriptures.

Change, Changed and Changing

Daniel was from a Christian home in Portland, Oregon, and had attended church his entire life. His parents had become believers in Jesus later in their early adult years and treasured their faith. Daniel had one sister and had attended Multnomah School of the Bible, graduating the year before. Priscilla often wondered if he really was single and unattached because surely the other young ladies at Multnomah found his appearance and character just as attractive as she did. However, short of the occasional comments about his friends from church, he never gave her any reason to believe he was not serious about continuing to pursue a relationship with her. His honesty in the letters kept pouring out who he was and what was important to him. Since he was seven, Daniel's mother had been ill with cancer. His father had worked hard for years on a family farm in North Dakota and taught Daniel the value of a responsible work ethic. Daniel was very careful with his money, almost too frugal at times.

He was working as a school bus driver while he raised financial support to return to Chicago to work full-time on the near west side with families living in high-rise projects. His fundraising included opportunities for him to meet with members of his church in their homes and tell them about the ministry he believed God had called him to do and invite them to partner with him in prayer or regular financial support.

The simple white envelopes began to show up more regularly in Priscilla's mailbox. One day there was a smart-looking picture of this Daniel in a bright red tie, a shy smile under his blue eyes. She rather liked the picture, because that one meeting of three hours back in July had been awfully short to continue to remember the finer features of this person she was beginning to really care about. It seemed so safe to be able to write letters back and forth without the physical distraction of being around each other in person. Matters of the heart were discussed such as struggles, temptations, victories and fears. Priscilla kept noticing that whenever there was any issue that was discussed, Daniel's first resort was to go to God in prayer. It seemed like it was completely natural for him;

something he had done or observed his whole life. She continued to keep their friendship somewhat of a secret, not fully trusting the rest of the world to not judge her for following him to Chicago.

One of the commitments Priscilla had made before coming to Chicago was that she intended to work on her college degree. She kept meeting people from Moody Bible Institute and many of the programs at the mission were staffed by MBI students who were learning how to do practical Christian ministries in various church programs throughout the city.

Priscilla had one haunting fear from the time she first learned of the birds and the bees when she was sixteen. Because she learned about the horrors of rape in the same conversation about where babies came from, she was terrified that she would be raped someday. Her mother went on to tell her in that same conversation that if she lived a pure life and did not do anything sinful to attract men to her, she would never have to worry about being raped. She continued to have nightmares though, waking up just before it happened out of breathtaking fear. It was an odd fear, because she was not around anyone in her family or community who had broken her trust. Any man she had been around, especially her father, was respectful to her and never took advantage of her in any way.

Upon moving to Chicago, Priscilla was eager to visit the Moody Bible Institute, about which she had heard and read for years. She loved the heroes who had gone out across the globe as missionaries and was delighted when she finally had the opportunity to walk under the arch and through the same halls which they had walked. She boldly enrolled in several classes with one of her new friends in the office and they would ride together to the campus after work, have a tasty sandwich supper in The Cove, and head to class. Priscilla absolutely loved every class and professor. She was gulping down what she learned as quickly as she possibly could. It felt like she would learn about a theory in her class and return to her home, the laboratory, to put everything into practice.

However, Priscilla was not prepared for the little plaque she saw on the wall of the Practical Christian Ministry office. This was where the students gathered to coordinate their assignments out in the city doing ministry in churches, youth centers or for street evangelism. There was a picture of a beautiful young girl, college aged, who had been raped and murdered on her way to her assignment within a few miles of the institute. Priscilla was shocked. Everything she had thought she could believe of her mother's theory about good girls being safe suddenly did not seem believable.

She continued to have her bad dreams and wondered sometimes why she had felt so assuredly called to come and work in Chicago when she was too afraid of the dark to go out to the alley and empty the kitchen wastebasket while she lived at home. She was not prepared for the fact that when she took a risk in faith, God would protect her and walk with her straight into her greatest fear. It miraculously melted away.

Later that winter on an ordinary night, she was curled up in her tiny bedroom on the second floor in her apartment. Her roommate was out of town and she was there alone. She heard a slight disturbance in the alley behind her bedroom window but thought nothing of it as she was getting more and more used to the constant hum of city commotion. Several days later she learned that the pastor and his wife's home on the corner had been broken into and she had been raped. Priscilla was broken-hearted to think of this crime happening to such a dear person. Strangely, though, Priscilla knew she would fear no evil, for even though she walked in the valley of the shadow of death God would be with her and his rod and staff would comfort her. (Psalm 23) From that day forward she never had another nightmare about being raped.

It helped Priscilla's sense of direction for the city of Chicago to be laid out on a grid due to its perfect, flat topography. She learned that after the incident of Mrs. O'Leary's cow knocking over the lantern and starting the great Chicago fire of 1871, the city had been rebuilt in a logical map. Once the major streets were memorized, Priscilla could usually find her way around any neighborhood just by an intuitive logic that told her east from west. After all, any eastbound traffic eventually would end up in the lake. One dark night she found herself in an unfamiliar place, driving among tall buildings with no streetlights and many faces she could hardly see in the dim lighting. Suddenly she recognized that she was lost and that she probably looked very out of place in her little, white, Toyota Starlet, toodling about with her white face aglow. It was almost uncanny how quickly she made her way back to familiar territory and was reminded once again that God was always with her.

On an ordinary day in February, after Valentine's Day had come and gone, an unexpected surprise arrived on the third-floor administrative offices of Inner City Impact. There was a beautiful bouquet of spring flowers (not red roses) delivered by a florist and it was clearly not to be construed as a Valentine's Day token from an overzealous lover. The words on the card were innocuous enough with the generic term "Thinking of You". They were from Daniel and the cat was out of the bag! She could no longer keep everyone from knowing that there had been a connection seven months earlier at the gathering on the west side of Chicago, and these two may have only met for three hours, but they had not forgotten each other. In fact, they were getting to know each other better with every passing letter.

A few days later, it was time for the wedding of Terry, her dear roommate. It was a beautiful affair, with an elegant, vintage style that came together effortlessly at the hands of the creative and thrifty bride. They were married at her little church in the neighborhood which she attended with the young high-school students with whom she worked. Her husband was full of character, a hardworking and just happened to be Daniel's roommate in Chicago the summer before.

It was then time for Priscilla to move to a different apartment and she was blessed with an attractive brownstone in Logan Square. There on the first floor she shared an apartment with another creative missionary and together they served the third-fifth grade girls in their neighborhood. She learned a lot from this Chicago native and loved the architecture of the apartment with its hardwood floors, white built-ins and lovely, beveled-glass bay window. Her homemaking skills increased when her cousin and an old friend from grade school brought back the remainder of her belongings and she was able to set up housekeeping with her own canopy bed, dresser, books and sewing machine.

It was into this setting that Daniel would soon be getting to know her face to face, because he had raised his support to be a full-time missionary in Chicago, had paid off his car and his college debt and was due to arrive in June 1990. Priscilla continued to receive telephone calls and letters from another friend in Atlanta. Another Daniel had captured her attention through a contact at Compassion

International, Inc., and they had continued to keep in touch with each other. She told him honestly about the Daniel in Oregon and she reported to the Daniel in Oregon about the Daniel in Atlanta and told them both that they were fair game. Only time would tell.

Love Birds Fly

Daniel from Oregon drove across the country, arriving in Chicago early in the summer as planned. Priscilla's anticipation now exceeded all life events which had transpired up to this point. It seemed she had waited so long and tried so hard to hide her eagerness. Just as she was returning to her desk in the office, there he was in the hallway; tall, smiling, brown curls, wearing a sweatshirt with a whale's tail on the front. His timid eyes, however, averted her glance. He had come to take her to lunch as previously planned.

It was delightful to talk in person after ten months of letters and phone calls. The local deli offered tasty sandwiches and chips and it even seemed a bit nostalgic to be riding in a Plymouth Volare again since Priscilla had learned to drive in the same make and model. They decided to plan a first "real date" later in the week: dinner at Dapper's East with a walk along Lake Michigan and through Lincoln Park to follow.

With anticipation and some serious trepidation, Priscilla prepared for Daniel to pick her up for their date. She had called her parents to update them that Daniel had arrived in town and told her father that if he had any advice for her, now would be the time to give it because she could tell she was going to really fall for him when they started to date in person. Her daddy told her he expected her to keep a curfew and always be in no later than eleven o'clock at night. He also reminded her that "nothing good happens after midnight" and that any dating that needed to be done could be handled in daylight hours. Priscilla agreed to his terms because of how much she loved and respected her father.

The dinner at Dapper's East was tasty and to their mutual surprise, both showed up with a Bible, a pen and a journal, without prior arrangement. They both wanted to go over each other's expectations and define the relationship so there would be no misunderstandings. Priscilla was especially concerned that she not make the same mistake twice after assuming that the friend she had from the Air Force might be interested in her romantically someday. She wanted to know Daniel's intentions right up front and not waste either their affections or time.

After dinner and conversation, they headed down to the lakefront to see the fountain and stroll through the park. At one point, Daniel reached down and took her hand to be sure she would not fall as they walked under some bridges and tunnels along the way. Priscilla appreciated that kindness and found it easy to trust him.

Meanwhile, the other Daniel in Atlanta continued to call and keep in contact with Priscilla, checking to see how her missionary work was progressing and asking about Daniel from Oregon as well. It was becoming increasingly difficult for Priscilla to decide who to keep. They were both different and had specific strengths that the other did not have. It came right down to their differing careers. Would she be content as the wife of an information technology professional from the south or would inner city ministry with a man who also loved children be more fitting?

The summer brought many happy memories, including a firework display down on the lakefront where Priscilla wore shorts for the first time in her life. She seemed to be the only one for miles around who never wore shorts and it was desperately hot in

Chicago's midsummer. She selected a pair of pink, seersucker shorts for her evening date and to their complete delight, the fireworks show ended with a double heart above the lake. She knew it was just for them!

Late August brought a surprise when the two stopped near Columbus Park in Little Italy. There was a gentle rain, and Daniel held an umbrella for Priscilla as they made their way through the park. Along a side street with brick apartment buildings and wrought iron fences, toward the courtyard of a Catholic church, they strolled in the rain. Across the courtyard from the church were some steps so they decided to sit down. Daniel said, "There is something I have been wanting to tell you for a long time. I love you. And I have brought this to help you know it is true." With that, he dipped into a bag on his left and pulled out a long-stemmed red rose, giving it to her. He also had two Dove ice cream bars in his bag and shared them with her as well.

September included a camping trip with Priscilla's roommate to the Indiana Dunes State Park. Daniel was coming as well and joining her roommate's church event for the weekend It was a huge struggle for Priscilla to buy a swimsuit, let alone put it on and feel comfortable wearing it in public. They would be at a lakeside and others would be camping there as well, with their tents. She was going with her roommate to keep up good relations and mutual respect with her and she and her roommate shared a tent together.

One evening, Priscilla and Daniel decided to go on a walk just as the stars were starting to come out. They were circling a small lake that was surrounded with pine trees, dark against the deep twilight sky. Sliding towards the horizon was a beautiful, crescent moon. It was there that Daniel paused and looked Priscilla in the eyes to say, "Don't you think this would be a beautiful place for our first kiss?" Priscilla did not know what to say. They had already decided they would not kiss until they were engaged. Though both had briefly dated before meeting each other, neither had ever kissed. To her surprise, they barely knew how but figured it out. Priscilla was secretly thankful that her memory of their first kiss was so beautiful compared to a picnic they had earlier in the summer when two drug dealers dived out of a bush nearby with a wad of cash. This seemed more pleasing aesthetically than that did on a hot and sticky afternoon.

As the fall schedule rolled out and the staff worked with the children in weekly after-school clubs, camping trips, small groups and special activities, Daniel settled into his full-time role working with the fourth, fifth and sixth-grade boys. Priscilla continued to try to meet the growing expectations of her position assisting the Executive Director. Board meeting preparation was always the hardest when she received her materials at the last minute but tried to compile them perfectly on time. This effort often kept her late into the evening in the third-floor office by herself.

The cool evening air blowing in off Lake Michigan promised a change of seasons as winter approached. Daniel and Priscilla had a few rare evenings out in the suburbs to shop and Daniel suggested they look at rings. Priscilla tried, but she couldn't get excited. So much guilt and fear overwhelmed her at the thought of so permanently going against the way she had been brought up. Since wearing gold had been prohibited, she felt overwhelmed by the options. They chose to stroll through the local nearby grocery store instead, a much less threatening activity.

One special highlight of every week was a Bible study with a group of single and college-aged students in the Chicago area through The Navigators organization. It was a true means of encouragement to her spiritually. Priscilla made new friends and was thankful for the accountability and the opportunities to learn more about her new home, surrounded by them. Thanksgiving was coming and Priscilla and her roommate decided that all the Bible Study friends who could not go home for the holiday would be invited to their apartment for dinner. She asked her mother for directions about how to prepare a traditional Thanksgiving dinner and her mother replied with a detailed, handwritten explanation of everything from stuffing the turkey to preparing a centerpiece.

The week before the planned celebration, the staff delivered Thanksgiving boxes to the families of the children they served. Churches provided the contents for the boxes because the missionaries knew where the needs were and delivered up and down the dark stairs of the high-rise projects for an entire Saturday. The walls were soft from the lichens that grew in the shadowy hallways where the darkness hung like a pall in the stairwells. The light bulbs were not replaced, the handrailing had been removed and sold for drugs.

Even so, Priscilla and Daniel's hearts were bright as they looked forward to a date planned for that evening. They were going to Edwardo's Pizza downtown near Moody Bible Institute. The walk through the city alone was enjoyable and once there, the unmistakable aroma of genuine, Italian pizza with generous tomato sauce and thick cheese on a crunchy crust created a delightful memory. Daniel started acting a little anxious and excused himself once from the table to quickly return. Soon they were walking along the Chicago River with the backdrop of the city lights and the river walkway. Daniel knelt on the cobblestone pier, lowered one knee and asked Priscilla to be his wife. She responded, "Yes! It is a complete yes!" They knew they were officially engaged, sealing it with a kiss. Adding to the romance of the moment, a pesky rat darted across the pier and behind the building beside them. The ring came later the next week in a parking lot of a large park on the north side of town. Priscilla was still overwhelmed by the seriousness of her commitment and while expecting to be giddy with excitement as she broke the news to the world, she was slower and more deliberate about releasing this new information.

The next week she was preparing dinner for Daniel when she received a phone call from Atlanta's Daniel. In his faithful, optimistic attitude he was checking in, always supportive. She brought him up to date that Daniel was on his way over to celebrate their engagement for dinner. The doorbell was ringing as she hid in the walk-in pantry talking to him. He politely wished her well, kept in touch with them both through their engagement and wedding and silently slipped out of her life after.

Priscilla and Daniel's decision to work in Chicago, write letters to each other, date and become engaged was a very personal one for each of them. So firmly did they believe it was right that they had not even met each other's parents before their engagement. There had been communication by telephone and mail, but to sit down with each other face-to-face had to wait until December and February that winter.

Christmas with Priscilla's parents was magical with a record-breaking snow. Skiing at the Broadmoor and showing Daniel all her favorite haunts made Priscilla forget the many reasons she had wanted to leave. Priscilla's parents were gracious and accepting of their new son-in-law-to-be and made every effort to make him feel welcome. Before they even arrived, arrangements had been made for him to stay at a home elsewhere in the neighborhood, vigilantly guarding their purity for their wedding night.

Two months later, they flew together to Portland, Oregon, for Daniel to represent the urban ministry at the Bible college from which he had graduated. They were thankful for an opportunity to meet his side of the family with the financial assistance of their ministry as Daniel would be representing Inner City Impact at his alma mater's missions conference. Priscilla was not prepared for the way she met Daniel's parents. Whisked away by an outgoing brother-in-law-to-be, while Daniel tended a booth at the college, Priscilla was taken to their home without her beloved. It felt so awkward meeting them for the first time without him and she had no courage to stand up and refuse. She loved them both and began a lifelong friendship with his sister. It was such a privilege to spend time together as a family and to visit the church where Daniel had grown up since he was in the nursery.

A generous wedding shower was given by the people of the church and many gifts were packed for returning to Chicago. Being young and naive, Priscilla and Daniel did not think through the logistics of how they would safely get the cargo to their separate apartments. Arriving in Chicago's O'Hare airport late in the night on a discounted flight, they took the El into the city and Daniel left Priscilla with all the gifts on the platform of the underground subway station in the middle of the night while he ran home in the dark to get his car. They noticed Daniel's mother was frail but did not realize that she would be leaving them within the year.

In April, Priscilla's friends started talking about having a lingerie shower for her. First of all, what was that? Second of all, how could she even endure it, coming from her modest background? She decided once again that she needed to be strong and adjust to the many changes in her surrounding culture. Most of the friends were very understanding and considerate in their gifts. One former missionary from Guatemala simply gave a beautiful neck scarf instead of embarrassing her dear friend. That simple gesture of understanding meant a lot to Priscilla.

May came and with it the sweet sound of ringing wedding bells. Priscilla flew home early for the final details of the linen wedding dress her mother had made for her. It included a lovely chapel veil and circle of white flowers as a headpiece. Many of her friends from Compassion got together to give Priscilla a very meaningful bridal shower at the home of her neighbor. There were friends going back to third grade in attendance and it was a time of much love and fond memories. Each gift meant the world to Priscilla, because it represented a person who had a great impact on her life. She was extremely thankful every time she saw one in her home thereafter.

Priscilla had lost a significant amount of weight with all the excitement and her dear mother had to remodel the wedding dress to correctly fit her within a week. She patiently took apart the side seams and redid everything to be custom-designed for Priscilla. Daniel's parents came down from Oregon with a registered nurse to accompany his very ill mother. Family and friends helped host all the guests and Daniel stayed at the neighbor's home before the wedding. He awoke the morning of the wedding anxious and sad about the condition of his mother.

He had never seen her so sick before. Priscilla asked him to bring down his shoes and leave them on the front porch since they did not want to see each other before the ceremony on their wedding day. She polished them with much love and returned them to the porch for Daniel to pick up while she went to the church to get ready for the wedding.

Frank kindly went on one final mission of love that hearkened back to the days of childhood. He took a trip out to a little town in the foothills with the many jugs he had saved to collect "Manitou Water" as the mineral water was called. They were mixed it with pink lemonade to share at the wedding reception for about three hundred people.

The photographer Daniel and Priscilla selected for their wedding was the same one responsible for photographing and cataloguing all the children's photos for the sponsors with Compassion International, Inc. He generously provided his time as a gift to the couple, handing them four rolls of film when he was finished.

Four dear friends stood up with each of them along with four little children. Some of Priscilla's cousins and relatives would not take part in the wedding because of the exchange of rings that they had chosen with no guilt. The neighbor did all the flowers for the wedding. The cake was beyond her fondest dreams. The wedding was filled with joy and biblical wisdom for a lasting marriage and crowned with a sweet song which they sang to each other written by Steve Green - "Cherish the Treasure".

Friends had gotten together to decorate for the reception, and it was absolutely beautiful. White lattice, grapevine intertwined hearts woven with flowers and flickering votives set a cozy atmosphere for greeting every guest.

As they left for Denver that evening to begin their honeymoon, there was contentment and peace in each other's company. Truly, after delighting in the Lord, He had given them the desires of their hearts.

"Delight thyself also in the Lord: and he shall give thee the desires of thine heart" (Psalm 37:4).

Acknowledgments

My favorite part of this book is acknowledging the people who helped bring the project to completion. Most importantly, I thank my Savior for bringing salvation to me and leading me through confusing and frightening situations yet never leaving my side. On earth, I have a picture of this in my husband, David Gemar, who has lovingly encouraged my writing and tediously read every word, checking for errors. Twice.

Our daughters have been supporters in unique ways. Always encouraging, they have left me alone to write or helped me work out a difficult passage when I had no creativity left. Grace read parts of my manuscript and cheered me on while Kathleen handed down her refurbished MacBook for the final formatting and completion of my work.

In my writing quest I have had a precious gift in a friend and accountability partner, Nancy Williams. She has prayed with and for me, written with me in coffee shops, accompanied me on writing retreats and brought me calming sprigs of her homegrown lavender. I do not know how I could have made it to the finish line without her faithful friendship.

During the final year of writing, my Aunt Kathleen, who lives with us in her senior years, has been a loyal helper. Her busy hands have washed dishes and folded laundry, helping me steal extra minutes out of my busy days. Along with her daily caregivers, our home has been maintained beautifully. It was into her hands that I placed the first paper manuscript and she read it thoroughly that very evening.

My proofreaders and editors have been invaluable in catching mistakes and seeing areas where I could improve. For Pamela Johnson, Qat Wanders, Ellen DeLatte, Angela Eagan, Olive Hall and Bonnie Stewart, I am extremely thankful. And to all my readers out there, I welcome your input if you find a mistake! It will hound me for eternity if I know there is something incorrect that could have been fixed. Chautona Havig saved me at the last minute with proper formatting.

The artwork on the cover was designed by our son-in-law, Alex Cook, who took two pictures to create the composite. One was the church where my parents met and were married, where my sister graduated from high-school and where I spent my last day in school before the church split. The other picture was of the farmhouse in which I attended Bible school in the Midwest. He artfully interposed them to demonstrate some of the memories that surrounded those years of my life.

The process of self-publishing is not for the faint of heart, but I received excellent instruction through Self-Publishing School and would encourage any other emerging authors to consider their excellent curriculum. My writing coach in Scotland, Ramy Vance, was a wealth of knowledge and encouragement. Weekly direction from Sean Summers and the founder of SPS, Chandler Bolt, kept me on track and increased my understanding of the process. For a discount on the cost of the course, see the coupon.

SELF-PUBLISHING SCHOOL GOLDEN TICKET

HELP YOUR FRIEND GET THE BEST POSSIBLE PRICING ON SPS WHEN YOU SEND THEM OUR WAY!
(THEY GET $250 OFF, AND YOU GET $250)

FUTURE STUDENT: BOOK A CALL WITH US TODAY AT: SELF-PUBLISHINGSCHOOL.COM/APPLY

Barbara Gemar _____ TOLD ME ABOUT SPS.

ADMIT ONE: ONE LIFE CHANGED BY WRITING A BOOK!

My acknowledgements would not be complete without the mention of two significant teachers in high school and college: Charlotte Carroll Halbert and Mary Vernon (deceased). These teachers inspired me and ignited a spark of writing within that burns brightly to this day.

A Closing Letter

Dear Reader,

Thank you for reading my story. Parts of it were very difficult to write, but the one thing that compelled me to complete it was YOU. If there is any part of this book that resonates with you because of your own bondage in the past or even in the present, please take heart!

You can tell God how you feel. Ask Him to guide you or bring you to someone who can help you put your faith in Him. Read the Bible and God will draw you to Him. "A Christian is someone who believed they are innately sinful and can do nothing about it unless they accept that Jesus sacrificed himself and rose again for them." – Daniel Cook

Galatians 5:1 says: "Stand fast therefore in the liberty wherewith Christ hath made us free, and be not entangled again with the yoke of bondage."

Because of Jesus,
Barbara

P.S. If you would like to be updated on future works, please go to my web page at AReadyWriter.ink, sign up for my newsletter, and I will send you a digital copy of the original artwork for this book cover to express my appreciation.